CONTENTS

WHEN THE BLUE SHIFT COMES

ROBERT SILVERBERG

SEQUEL NOVELLA BY
ALVARO ZINOS-AMARO

THE STELLAR GUILD SERIES
TEAM-UPS WITH BESTSELLING AUTHORS

MIKE RESNICK
SERIES EDITOR

an imprint of

MANOR
Rockville, Maryland

Series edited by Mike Resnick.

ISBN: 978-1-61242-074-5

www.PhoenixPick.com
Great Science Fiction & Fantasy
Free Ebook every month

Published by Phoenix Pick
an imprint of Arc Manor
P. O. Box 10339
Rockville, MD 20849-0339
www.ArcManor.com

WHEN THE BLUE SHIFT COMES

A Greeting From the Series Editor

Welcome to another Stellar Guild book, the ultimate pay-it-forward science fiction series. Most of the field's superstars can't pay back the people who helped them when they were starting out; those people are rich, or dead, or both. So, in this field more than any other, it is traditional to pay forward.

Stellar Guild was created for just that purpose. Each book in the series consists of a novella by one of the field's long-established superstars, plus a novelette by a protégé of the star's own choosing.

When the Blue Shift Comes presents a novella by one of the field's true giants, Robert Silverberg—Worldcon Guest of Honor, Nebula Grand Master, multiple Hugo winner, multiple Nebula winner, international bestseller. And for his protégé, he has chosen Alvaro Zinos-Amaro, who has already established himself as a top-notch critic and reviewer, and is now ready to move into fiction in a major way.

Prior Stellar Guild books have featured Kevin J. Anderson, Mercedes Lackey, and Harry Turtledove and their protégés—and don't go away, because we have Larry Niven, Eric Flint, and others (and their protégés) under contract.

Mike Resnick

WHEN THE BLUE SHIFT COMES

Book One
THE SONG OF LAST THINGS

ROBERT SILVERBERG

So when this world's compounded union breaks,
Time ends, and to old Chaos all things turn,
Confused stars shall meet....

—Marlowe, *Lucan's Pharsalia*

THE SONG OF LAST THINGS FIRST:
FOUR QUICK CANTOS

1.

HEIGH-HO! IT'S TIME TO SING of the ending of time! Yes, the death of worlds, the crumbling of the continuum, the great Folding-In of the Gloriously Unfolded. Here is how it came about: this is what befell in the Time of the Falling of the Stars, which led to the Crossing of the Dark, which brought about the Birth of the Universe. For what we are gathered here to pay homage to today is the Grand Circularity of Everything.

First things first and last things last, that's the way of the worlds—but also last things first, as you will be amply shown. That's how it always goes: how it always has gone, how it always must. The cosmos is a serpent with its tail in its mouth, and who is to say which is the beginning and which the end? Not I, not you, not any of us.

2.

—IF THE SONG HAS NO BEGINNING and no end, where shall we start?

—Why not start, for the sake of starting somewhere, with the planet that once was called Earth, and will be called Earth again in distant times to come? We will be visiting that

Earth-to-come in a little while. We'll stop off at a couple of other places first; but Earth-to-come is our real destination. *Earth's* destination is another matter altogether.

3.

YOU KNOW WHERE EARTH IS. The third planet of a small-ish middle-aged yellowish sun in the Milky Way galaxy, etc., etc. You probably call it Earth, yes, but some of your neighbors on your little planet call it La Tierra and others know it as Die Erde and still others as La Terre, and so on and so on, a hundred different names for the good old Mondo simultaneously in use all around the globe, there where you sit in the early twenty-first century, as such things are tallied under the widely prevalent Christian way of counting such units. (Though your twenty-first century also happened to be the fifteenth century of Islam and the fifty-ninth century by Hebrew reckoning, just to name a couple of the calendars that are currently functioning in the era when you live.)

But in the middle years of the Ninth Mandala everyone has swung around to calling it Earth again. They find it amusing to revive the dear old name after so many thousands of centuries of neglect.

The Ninth Mandala, which is the era where we choose to enter our story, lies at a time extremely far in the future. That's the first displacement adjustment you need to make. There will be more.

4.

HOW FAR IN THE FUTURE? Very far. I can't be more precise than that. All I can tell you is that we're going to be looking in on the year 777 of Cycle 888 of the 1111th Encompassment of the Ninth Mandala.

What does that mean? Not much, to me, to you. Heigh-ho! A long time from now, that's what it means, and more than that I can't really say. But even at this distance we are able to see, through the mists of immense time, various people of that era in their various characteristic attitudes.

We have a hero—however reluctant he may be to play that part. We have a heroine, certainly. We may even have a villain or two—for there's still a little villainy around in the highly civilized Ninth Mandala.

Here's our unwilling hero: Hanosz Prime of Prime, thinking about giving up the ownership of a world.

Here's our heroine, Sinon Kreidge's lovely daughter Kaivilda, waiting for Hanosz Prime to come for a visit and change the course of history, among other things.

Here's grim old Sinon Kreidge himself, thinking—to his very great surprise—about the possibility that he may finally have to die.

Those are some of the people whose stories we sing here. They happen to be immortal, by the way, all but Hanosz Prime, who was born on the wrong planet. The other two are Earthfolk, and immortality is one of the little bonuses of life on Earth in the 1111th Encompassment of the Ninth Mandala. The whole universe envies the Earthfolk their freedom from death, but nowhere else has the trick been managed. On all the other worlds, people live for a merely stupendous span of time, measured not in decades but in centuries. On Earth, though, they long ago stopped having to die at all.

But it is late, very late, in the cosmic scheme of things. The fun is beginning to come to a stop. The End of All Creation is approaching, actually. The Time of the Falling of the Stars is at hand.

Heigh-ho! It is the ultimate disaster. Let us sing, for what else is there to do? Scratch? Sleep? Cry?

Heigh-ho!

An Occurrence at Vyeptos Station

THERE'S NOBODY HUMAN AT VYEPTOS STATION. There isn't even anybody alive there. It's just an automatic free-orbit monitoring outpost, somewhere out in the dark airless midst of the Milky Way, a goodly distance from Earth.

It was put there long ago—in Sixth Mandala times, it was—for some reason that nobody remembers or cares about any longer, and there it still is, eternally gliding through the endless night, traveling from nowhere to nowhere. It looks like a gigantic silvery bug, with many-faceted golden eyes sticking out here and there, measuring and recording this and that. Among the things that Vyeptos Station monitors is the Gravitational Constant. It also checks on the Interstitial Electromagnetic Current, the Mean Plasmatic Pressure, the Universal Ionization Factor, the Intergalactic Fog Quotient, and a number of other such details. It keeps track of the depth of the Galactic Abyss, measures the relative positions of the various adjacent galaxies, and takes the measure of the Total Mass of the Galaxy. It does all this a thousand times a day.

A thousand times a day, also, the automatic devices at Vyeptos Station encode their data and beam it toward listening posts on ten thousand different worlds, one of them the world that once again is called Earth. The information that Vyeptos Station has been sending out with such inexhaustible diligence since the remote era of the Sixth Mandala is duly recorded, entered in the archives of this world and that one, and—generally—ignored.

Occasionally someone does look at the input coming from Vyeptos Station. Those who do eventually notice one very odd fact: the figure for Total Mass of the Galaxy has been diminishing ever so slightly since the station's earliest days. Each measurement indicates the presence of a few atoms less than the one before. No one is quite sure why that should be, though there have been many speculative theories. It isn't regarded as cause for alarm—not to those who stop to consider how many atoms the galaxy contains. They feel pretty confident that it can spare a few, and maybe more than a few.

But Vyeptos Station, though it has no intelligent mind on board and certainly is unaware of its own reason for existing, nevertheless is equipped to emit danger signals when things seem to be heading in a dangerous direction, even if the recipients of its information aren't paying much attention to what it has to say. Since the days of the Sixth Mandala it has dutifully been taking note of the daily disappearance of a handful of atoms from the galaxy-at-large. Vyeptos Station isn't worried about that. Vyeptos Station isn't programmed to worry about anything. But it *is* programmed to do its job. And the cumulative and aggregate loss of mass has by this time crossed a certain predesignated threshold level. There are signs of a spectral blue-shift within the galaxy, too: local indications of the motion of matter toward the galactic center. It's time to send out word of trouble.

So on a certain day in the 1111th Encompassment of the Ninth Mandala, Vyeptos Station broadcasts a little distress signal:

CAUTION. GALACTIC MASS DETERIORATION HAS
NOW REACHED LEVEL FOUR INTENSITY.
CAUTION. CAUTION. CAUTION.

It sends that signal far and wide for twenty-four Galactic Standard Hours, as it was told to do long ago.

Then it stops doing so, and goes back to its regular routine of gathering information and tabulating numbers.

Vyeptos Station has just told anybody who's listening that the destruction of the galaxy that contains Earth is now a certainty. Certain confirmations have been ascertained and the process is not going to halt until the entire galaxy has been consumed, one atom at a time. The process is very likely going to continue indefinitely, as a matter of fact, and sooner or later the entire rest of the universe will suffer the same fate. This is not something about which Vyeptos Station is seriously concerned. Vyeptos Station, by its very nature, doesn't give a damn about the larger implications of the information it collects.

The question is: Does anybody else?

Hanosz Prime Is Feeling Old

THE NIGHT BEFORE HE DECIDED to be reborn for the second time, Hanosz Prime of Prime dreamed of howling whirlwinds and fields of fire-thistles, voices speaking out of the face of the sun, rivers of hot flame flowing through the streets of the capital city of the planet of which he was sole proprietor and hereditary absolute monarch.

(That's a fine and fancy name: Hanosz Prime of Prime. Fine and fancy, yes, a resonant treasure handed down across the centuries in his family to the eldest sons of the eldest sons. His birth-name actually was Hanosz Algolom Zeptilov Lebilak Gamifon Zwee plus a long string of binary numbers; but ever since he had inherited his title, a little more than a century ago, everyone had called him simply Hanosz Prime, or just Prime. And so will we.)

He was awake when he had the dream, for sleep as we understand the concept was long obsolete in Hanosz Prime's era. But it was a dream all the same, and a very disturbing one indeed: like an ancient curse returning, like an old disease flaring up anew. He had been much afflicted by violent dreams, disjointed and bewildering, when he was younger, in both his previous lives: strange spirals and whorls of light, stars dancing in the sky, comets disappearing into a well of blackness, and more. But this was the first time in years that any such tempestuous vision had troubled his mind. And if he had needed anything more to convince himself that it was time to be reborn again, that dream was sufficient.

He had been feeling old and weary for some time now. As well he should, you might think, considering that he had already lived two hundred years and a little over.

But in fact Hanosz Prime was still a young man, as age was reckoned in the 1111th Encompassment of the Ninth Mandala: a lifetime that had covered only a couple of hundred years so far wasn't very much, really. On his world—Prime, it was called, some seven hundred thousand parsecs away, one of several million extragalactic planets that had been colonized by settlers from Earth and her daughter worlds quite some time back (it was in the 513th Encompassment of the Seventh Mandala: that long ago!)—on his world, as I was saying, people often lived three thousand years, or even seven thousand, as Hanosz Prime's grandfather had.

That doesn't mean that there was any easy escape from the aging process for those people, even so. To remain youthful you had to undergo the rebirth process at regular intervals—that is to say, you had to go through the whole unpleasant dreary affair of growing old and then flush your body clear of the poisons of age—about once a century, say—to make it new and young again. You could do that over and over: up to a certain point, anyway. (Unless you happened to live on Earth, in which case you could keep going indefinitely, at least until now.)

So Prime, though still quite young in Ninth Mandala terms, had already had the experience of growing old a couple of times in his two hundred years. And—to borrow a line from a wise man of our own era—Prime hadn't liked getting old any more than you will.

(The difference between Prime's situation and yours or mine is that he was spared the whole nasty business of sagging flesh and spreading waistlines and blurry eyesight and graying hair and hardening arteries, because Prime had the good fortune to live in the Ninth Mandala, when hair and arteries were obsolete concepts and all the other manifestations of bodily decay that you see around you every day were kept in check by nifty homeostatic processes of automatic bioenergetic correction. Growing old, for Hanosz Prime and his friends and neighbors, was more of an inward matter: a growing creakiness of the soul, a corrugation of the psyche, a stiffening of the spiritual synapses. They would start to feel sour and petty and crabbed. Life would lose its joy and its juice. Physically, they could still do pretty much anything that they had been able to do when they were young; but they no longer *felt* like doing it.)

(That was what they understood as being old. It was a lousy way to be. So they did something about it. They provided themselves with a brand new lease on life.)

And now—the old turbulent dream of his youth coming back to haunt him anew, the whirlwinds and fire-thistles and mysterious voices and rivers of fire—the return of the grim hallucinations that had polluted his repose long ago—

If all *that* was going to start up again, Hanosz Prime decided, he had better see to it that he was young enough to withstand it.

"Prepare the tank," Hanosz Prime said to his high advisers and counselors. "Tonight I go in."

They looked at each other in dismay: for anything could happen, anything at all, while someone was in the rebirth tank. But they too had known the time for Hanosz Prime's next rebirth was coming near; and now it had arrived, and there was nothing they could do about it. For Hanosz Prime had issued his decree; and on the world called Prime, the word of Hanosz Prime was law.

(You learned just a moment or two ago that Earth is in mortal peril, up ahead there in the 1111th Encompassment of the Ninth Mandala. Doubtless you want to know more about that, now that I've caught your interest, and are wondering what we're doing seven hundred thousand parsecs away—in an adjacent galaxy, as a matter of fact, the one we call the Andromeda Nebula—stopping off on the planet called Prime in the Parasol System to explore the problems of an elderly king named Hanosz Prime who is having bad dreams.)

(But there's not that much of a hurry, actually: doomsday for Earth is still some time off, and I have good and sufficient reasons for wanting you to meet Hanosz Prime first, on his native turf. He's going to be deeply involved in Earth's problems, whether he wants to be or not.)

(So let's not go to Earth right away. Let's back up a little in space and time, instead, and come in on some events on the planet called Prime, in the Parasol system, off in the Andromeda Nebula, seven hundred thousand parsecs away.)

Only a few days before Hanosz Prime's dream, a traveler from a distant world passing through the Parasol system had stopped by to pay a courtesy call at the court, and had spoken of Earth to Hanosz Prime. So perhaps there was a connection. Perhaps it was the traveler's tales of the ancient world of Earth that had rekindled Hanosz Prime's fierce hallucinatory dreams.

"And then," the traveler had said, after a lengthy recitation of the wonders and marvels he had seen in the course of his visits to eleven solar systems of three different galaxies, "Then I went to Earth—"

"Earth?" Hanosz Prime said, feeling a faint flicker of wonder—for that was about as much wonder as he was capable of feeling, just then, age having taken its toll on him in the way that it had. "So it really exists?"

"Certainly it exists. Did you think it was only a myth?"

"There are some who think so, you know."

The traveler—his name was Zereshk Poloi, a native of Borani in the Ghasemi system—said, smiling a little, "Surely you speak in hyperbole, Hanosz Prime. Earth is definitely real. Earth is the great mother of us all, the fount and origin of our race."

"Yes. Yes. Of course it is."

"And therefore it *has* to exist. And does. I take it you haven't yet had an opportunity to visit the Old Galaxy at all, then?"

"I look forward eventually to the pleasure," said Hanosz Prime, somewhat sourly.

(This was a sore point for him; because, although Prime had traveled very widely indeed for a man of his age, he had lived only two lifetimes so far, which as you know was not very many at all in the Ninth Mandala. And so—although right at this moment he certainly felt ancient and weary and feeble and very ripe for rebirth—he was in actuality still an inexperienced boy, more or less, in Ninth Mandala terms. The contradiction bothered him. To have Zereshk Poloi slyly teasing him for being raw and unseasoned just at a time when he was struggling with the fatigue of age was profoundly offensive.)

But—though Prime was heartily bored with his guest by now—he maintained a proper facade of curiosity, and said, "Tell me about Earth, then. Is it beautiful, would you say?"

A gleam of excitement came into Zereshk Poloi's eyes. "You wouldn't believe how beautiful Earth is! It's beyond all comprehension. It's a wonderland—a fantasy. A planet in a billion. In ten billion!"

"How surprising," said Hanosz Prime languidly. "I would imagine it would be a weary, dreary, worn-out place. An eroded, abraded, used-up place, a dusty drab old hulk of a place."

"Ah, no, no, no! Its landscape is beyond compare! Its golden hills, its green valleys, its jewel-like lakes—I tell you, Hanosz Prime, everything you see is fresh and new and strange! The Earthfolk see to it that it is." He seemed lost in a rapture of glorious recollection. "The mist that hangs over the mountains—the shimmering colors of the air—the folds and convolutions of the landscape—oh, words fail me, Hanosz Prime. Words fail me! You simply have to see it for yourself."

"Indeed. Perhaps some day I will," said Hanosz Prime indifferently.

"An absolute paradise," cried Zereshk Poloi. "And its inhabitants—"

"Yes. Its immortal inhabitants." And Hanosz Prime sighed, for he felt anything but immortal himself these days. "What are they like, Zereshk Poloi?" he asked, forcing himself to make a show of interest, for politeness's sake.

"Grand lords and ladies, every one of them! So few in number—just a handful of them scattered widely over the face of the planet—and all of them so rich, so gloriously rich—all possibilities lie open to them! You want to cry for joy, seeing them living their wonderful lives on that wonderful world."

"To cry for joy," said Hanosz Prime. "Yes."

"I visited a dozen of them in their palaces. Lord Septa Septa—what a magnificent creature he is! And Lord Snape—Lord Klatre—you know the names?"

Hanosz Prime shook his head.

"But of all of them that I met, the most fascinating was Sinon Kreidge. A scholar—a connoisseur—a man of the highest breeding and refinement. He has a daughter—very few of them have offspring, you understand; but he does—a daughter named Kaivilda, of such delicacy and beauty and innate nobility that one feels privileged simply to stand in the same room as her. It is worth the voyage to the Old Galaxy just to meet Sinon Kreidge's daughter Kaivilda, that much I assure you. I suspect that to enter into rapport with her would be the experience of a lifetime."

"Indeed," said Hanosz Prime again, dispassionately. And felt older and wearier still, for he had lately lost all interest in entering into rapport with anyone, and the famous Kaivilda's delicacy and beauty and innate nobility tempted him not at all; but he could remember enough of what it was like to be young to feel saddened by the fact that Zereshk Poloi's rapturous description of the marvelous Kaivilda aroused not the slightest enthusiasm in him. He saw the traveler's excitement; he perceived his intense emotion. But he did not, could not, share it at all.

And now Prime had had enough of this chatter. Slowly, stiffly, he rose from his seat. Stiffly, slowly, he moved through the open door that led to the balcony of his royal palace. "Come," he said to Zereshk Poloi. "A little fresh air now, I think."

All the teeming complexity of the capital city lay spread out before them: orange-tiled roofs, glittering white stucco walls, towers of turquoise brick. It was a city of six million lively, energetic, ambitious, aggressive people. His subjects, yes. The thought of all those people out there, all those brawling, vigorous, insistent people, made old Hanosz Prime—old, though he had lived only two hundred years—feel like turning away and weeping.

"Earth," Zereshk Poloi said. "There's nothing like it! You've absolutely got to see it some day, Hanosz Prime. Such a beautiful world—such grand lords and ladies, leading such wondrous lives—"

"Grand lords and ladies," Hanosz Prime muttered. "Leading such wondrous lives. Which are never going to end. Grand lords and ladies who are destined to live forever, while we grow old and die. The bastards! I hate them all!"

And in high fury he spat over the balcony's edge as though hoping his spittle would travel all the way to Earth. It was the first show of any sort of real vitality that he had been able to muster in more days than he could remember.

Prime was certain then that he was just about ready for another rebirth. Such sourness and bitterness and dryness and general morbidity of soul, in the face of Zereshk Poloi's enraptured words and shining eyes—what else could it be, if not a sign that he was just about done with this current life of his? And his terrifying dream, a few nights later, clinched it for him. If the crazy mindstorms of his earlier days were going to come back to plague him again, he needed all the strength he could summon to defend himself against them.

And so here he is, now, descending into the rebirth tank.

(It took seventy or eighty years, generally, to reach the stage when you were ripe for rebirth. Then you climbed into a crystal tank and an intricate spiderweb of machinery enfolded you like a loving mother and you slipped off into sweet oblivion for a while, and when you awoke you were young again and ready to start all over. And could go on doing it and doing it, again and again, until eventually you arrived at the annoying point where the build-up of solar poisons in your system had at last become ineradicable under any circumstances, and that would be the end of you.)

(It was the radiation of your own sun that eventually did you in. The same benevolent sunlight that brings life brings death as well, a build-up of accumulated poisons that eventually could no longer be swept away. That was the unhappy case on all the worlds of all the galaxies where life was capable of happening. With one remarkable exception, as you already know.)

(It took two or three or sometimes even eight thousand years, if you were exceptionally lucky, to get to the point of irreversible decline. But when you did, further rebirth was impossible and you finally had to die, permanently and irrevocably, unless you lived on Earth. Everyone knew that and everyone accepted it with fairly good grace. Or tried to.)

And now Hanosz Prime of Prime—"Prime" for short—sole proprietor and hereditary absolute monarch of Prime of the Parasol system, sixty-fourth in direct descent from the Founder, has undergone his second trip to the rebirth tank at the age of 200-plus-a-little. Prime has arranged to be given a new and more youthful identity-matrix construct and to be placed inside a new and more ferocious-looking body-modularity during the course of the process.

(The custom, usually, was to have yourself transferred to a new body-modularity every time you entered a new identity-matrix. Very likely your old body would emerge from the tank in perfectly fine shape, but the chances were good that you had grown bored with it over the course of the last eighty or ninety years. And why carry an old modularity that bores you over into your brand new matrix?)

And here is Hanosz Prime, then, lying in the warm nutrients of the rebirth tank, returning to consciousness now after his latest rejuvenation. He opens his eyes, sits up, stretches, and looks around. He feels younger, yes. He feels cleansed and brightened and quickened. All the sluggishness and weight of age has been taken from him.

But what's *this*? he asks himself.

Strange thoughts are coursing through his rejuvenated mind. Strange emotions are assailing him. He finds himself at the center of an unexpected storm of furious feelings.

None of this is as it should be. Prime realizes that something has gone very wrong.

What Prime had been expecting was to come out of the tank feeling full of youthful vigor, pep, and zip. That was the whole point of the process.

But—as he stepped forth, rejuvenated and invigorated, glowing with health and vitality—he knew at once that somebody had miscalculated, that something had happened that should not have happened, that his entire mental outlook and fundamental personality had undergone a profound and radical shift during the course of the treatment. He wasn't simply young again. He was young and *different*. Very different.

The worst part was that he didn't give the slightest damn that he was. He was aware of what had happened—he hadn't changed *that* much. But it all felt perfectly okay to him.

It had certainly been about time, Prime had figured, for his next dip in the tank. For a long time now he had been feeling terribly old. And so he wanted to feel young again, of course. Why not?

But young and callow? Young and rash? Young and irresponsible? Young and—let's not mince words—young and foolish?

Young and totally unwilling to resume the ghastly boring task of being the sixty-fourth hereditary absolute monarch of Prime?

That was the essence of what had happened to him in the tank, this time around. It was altogether unanticipated and pretty damned explosive.

What had happened was that Prime, very suddenly, didn't want to be king any more. The urge to rid himself of all the dreary, endless, leaden responsibilities of high office was rampaging through his newly young neural network like a roaring river in high spate, cutting deep new gullies across a formerly placid plain.

Prime itched to turn his back on his native world and clear out—to head for some far corner of the cosmos where nobody would ever ask him again to sign a decree or proclamation, to attend the ceremonial launching of a new ship, to pin a medal on some glorious military hero.

He had ruled his not inconsiderable world, a place of grand valleys and lofty snow-capped mountains and beautiful meadows and thriving cities, for one hundred and ten years, which of course in our own very distant era used to be sufficient time to live an entire life, and then some. It was hard work, being Hanosz Prime of Prime, but he had been raised for the task and he carried it out with skill and devotion. During his time on the throne he had made many great decisions; he had held the power to loose and bind, and had used it forcefully and well; he had served his loving people with all his wisdom and all his heart.

And now he wanted nothing more than to chuck the whole damned business.

Let someone else be hereditary absolute monarch of this place, Prime found himself thinking, in the first ecstatic moments of his newest rebirth. *To hell with being Hanosz Prime of Prime. I've had enough.*

That wasn't supposed to happen. The rebirth process afforded psychological continuity; you came out basically the same person you were when you went in, but a lot more resilient, vigorous, open-minded, expansive, venturesome, and dynamic. That is to say, you retained the maturity and perspective you had acquired during the course of your life up to the point of rebirth, but when you entered your new matrix you were freed from the unavoidable sorry drag of negativistic attitudes that had come to entangle your increasingly weary psyche in the decades since your last session in the tank.

That was the way things were supposed to work, and that was how it had worked for Hanosz Prime the first time he had gone in for rebirth.

That was how he had figured it was going to work this time, too. But it hadn't.

All the high officials of the court, naturally, were in attendance on him in the moment of his emergence from the tank. They beamed, they fawned, they kowtowed, they did all the smoothly subservient things that high officials of absolute monarchs had been doing since the idea of kingship had been invented, a couple of billion years earlier and seven hundred thousand parsecs away, along the banks of the Tigris or the Euphrates or perhaps the Nile. Eagerly they awaited the first words to fall from the lips of the newly rejuvenated Hanosz Prime of Prime.

"Get my brother in here, and get him fast," is what those first words were. "I've got some very bad news for him."

A CONVERSATION AT KALAHIDE KEEP

ON EARTH, AT KALAHIDE KEEP, the grand estate of Sinon Kreidge, Sinon Kreidge sits brooding in his conjuratorium, pondering oblivion. To him, now, comes his daughter Kaivilda:

"I've been to the Plain, father. I've heard the Oracle speak."

He stares at her, with little show of interest.

"There is no reason for despair. A king who has no kingdom will come to us," Kaivilda tells him. "He will take the Earth on his shoulders and carry it to safety."

Sinon Kreidge continues to stare. His face is expressionless.

"This has no meaning for me," he says, finally. "Nothing can save us. Nothing, Kaivilda."

And he returns to his gloom.

Abdicating?

"—*abdicating*, Prime? But you can't! You absolutely can't! It's never been done. It's ridiculous. It's impossible. It isn't even constitutional!"

"It is now," said Hanosz Prime of Prime. "What's the sense of being the hereditary absolute monarch if I can't make unilateral proclamations? I'm quitting, and that's that. You're the new Prime of Prime. Or will be, the moment my abdication becomes effective."

"Which is when?" his brother asked, with symptoms of shock beginning to make themselves visible on his face.

"As soon as my ship leaves Prime's gravitational field," said Hanosz Prime of Prime. "I'll send you a signal when it does. And then—"

"No. I refuse."

"You're the heir presumptive, aren't you?"

"Well—"

"No sense dithering. You have to do it. Look: I clear out and am never seen again. The throne is vacant. You take over. It's that simple."

Prime's only brother—his formal name was Gililon Alahoom Tigibain Thrip and the usual binary digits, but everyone called him Prime Two—was sixty years younger than Prime, but he was also a little more than two thirds of the way through his current lifespan, which meant that he was definitely middle-aged just now and in no condition to have things of this sort dumped on him by his suddenly youthful and apparently berserk older brother. His eyes—there were five of them, arranged in a pentagram—filmed over with horror. His tendrils drooped. His genital escutcheon turned from bright crimson to a dejected pale green.

"No," he said again. "It's unthinkable."

"Maybe so. But you better start thinking it, though."

"I've had no training. I was never supposed to be doing this."

"Or anything else. I know. I sympathize deeply."

"*Prime!*"

"They'll be calling you that soon, won't they?"

Prime's brother was trembling with shock.

He begged, he moaned, he cajoled, he did half a dozen other highly unkingly things, while the high officers of the court watched with sickly expressions on their faces. But Prime was the absolute monarch, and so by definition his word was law. His sixty-four-times-removed ancestor, the greatly revered Founder, had quietly gathered up title to every scrap of the planet in the early days of the settlement and had taken total control of everything; and each of his heirs through the succeeding sixty-four generations had enjoyed the same unalloyed power. The Prime of Prime's word was inherently unchallengeable, and that was that. If Hanosz Prime wanted to step down from the throne, there was no way of preventing him from doing it.

"You were always a strange one," Prime Two said balefully. "They should have realized you were unstable before they ever made you the Prime. All those tortured dreams of yours—those weird jumbled visions—"

"Good," Prime said. "The world will be well rid of me, then. How nice for everyone to have a perfectly sane individual like you taking charge of things."

"I'm perfectly sane, yes," said Prime Two. "But I'm incompetent. As you bloody well know."

"Don't be so hard on yourself."

"I'm simply being realistic."

"Lack of self-esteem has always been a problem for you, hasn't it? I blame myself. But you may gain confidence with practice. A few years of wielding absolute power will work wonders for you, brother. Believe me, it will."

"Prime. Please. *Please.*"

"We've already been through the part of the discussion where you moan and beg. Let's not do it all over again."

"You really are serious about this, then."

"I really am," said Prime.

Prime Two stared. His mandibles worked wordlessly; his tendrils writhed themselves into knots; his four shoulders slumped as though they already felt the weight of the crown descending.

"Where will you go?" he asked, finally.

"I don't know. I just want to get away from here."

"But there's no sweeter world in all the universe," said Prime Two.

"Maybe so. I still want to get away."

Prime's decision, he said, was irrevocable. He signed a royal decree—his very last, he hoped—to that effect. And began making plans for his departure to points unknown, while the unfortunate Prime Two set about the hopeless task of learning how to become a king at extremely short notice.

There were a few moments in the succeeding weeks when Hanosz Prime wondered whether what he was about to do made any sense. But the answer always came quickly: it didn't *have* to make any sense. He was young again. By definition, then, he was immature. He felt restless and frivolous again. Good. That was what he was supposed to feel like, now that he was young again. And youth was a commodity too precious to waste in being a hereditary absolute monarch. Let Prime Two have the dreary job a while, Prime thought. He might just come to like it—and if not, why, they could always discuss switching things back again after a time. Say, in a century or two.

Prime still hadn't decided where he should go, though.

And then Mirza-Mirza Ghasemi, who was High Ambassador of Prime to several dozen worlds of the Old Galaxy—the modest star-cluster that had been the ancestral womb of the entire far-flung human race—returned from his latest diplomatic mission with some remarkable news.

"It seems that they've discovered an anomalous hole in the continuum out there," Mirza-Mirza Ghasemi told the newly rejuvenated Prime, "and it's very gradually expanding its zone of effective attraction. Apparently it's been there since the beginning of time, quietly growing larger as it gains energy, and it's become big enough now to be detected. The spectral lines of certain stars are being shifted toward the blue end in the vicinity of the anomaly, and strong gravitational-wave patterns are being observed, as well as unusual tidal effects in the fabric of interstellar space."

"Indeed," said Prime, who had had very little training in such matters as science. "And what does all that actually mean, if anything?"

"That it's been slowly eating everything within its reach for the past fifteen or twenty billion years, one atom at a time, and by now its reach is getting big enough to be significant. Some sort of critical threshold has been passed. The Old Galaxy is contracting as the hole feeds on it. Things are rushing toward each other. Entire sectors of space are being pulled into the anomaly. Four complete solar systems have been swallowed up already, suns and all, as a matter of fact. The process is continuing and will continue indefinitely. The more it eats, the hungrier it gets. All this is taking place, of course, several million light-years from here: there's no need for us to worry, your lordship. But the risk to certain parts of the Old Galaxy is considerably more immediate. They say that the system of which Earth is a part is getting troublesomely close to the hole as things contract, and Earth is very likely going to be drawn into the vortex of destruction in a relatively short time."

"Earth?" Prime said, in wonder. "The mother world itself, gobbled up by an anomalous hole?"

"So it would seem."

"My God! All that beauty gone! All those famous historical sites!" He could almost see Zereshk Poloi weeping with chagrin. And then another and more mischievous thought came to him: "And—my God—the Earthfolk themselves! They'll have to move out of their nice little nest, won't they? And that means they'll have to die, just like the rest of us!"

(A little shiver of the nasty but very widespread emotion known in our era as *Schadenfreude* rippled through Hanosz Prime as that realization struck him. *Schadenfreude* means the joy we feel upon learning of the misfortunes of others. And—listen, don't try to tell me that you aren't the sort of person who feels that way when you hear somebody else's bad news. Of course you are. Everybody enjoys a little *Schadenfreude*, except saints, and I'm not so sure they don't too.)

Prime laughed. "It must really be driving them wild," he said. "—How soon is this going to happen, anyway? A relatively short time, you said? *How* short?"

Shrugging, the ambassador said, "The calculations aren't really clear. One set of equations indicates the disappearance of Earth might happen as soon as the next two or three thousand years. A different astronomer says it's at least a million years away, or maybe more. And I understand there's another estimate that puts the time of the catastrophe somewhere in between. They're still arguing about it."

"But there's no doubt that it's going to happen, sooner or later?"

"Sooner or later, yes, definitely. So most Old Galaxy authorities are saying. Although they're arguing about that, too, I understand."

"They must be an argumentative bunch."

"So they are. But the consensus is that the disaster *will* happen. Earth will be destroyed. Not to mention a good deal of the universe in its vicinity. A messy business."

"Well, then," Prime said. "That answers a big question for me." Suddenly Zereshk Poloi's excited words were ringing in his mind, stirring him as they had not remotely been able to do while he was still old. What was it he had said about Earth? *A wonderland—a fantasy. A planet in a billion. In ten billion!* He summoned the high officials of the court, and his unhappy younger brother as well. "It's time," he told them. "Let's say our goodbyes. I leave tomorrow."

"And have you decided where you intend to go?" asked Prime Two.

"Yes. To Earth," Prime said.

A Little Essential
Background Information

YOU MAY HAVE NOTICED those puzzling references to Prime's brother's mandibles and drooping tendrils, his five eyes, and other such features. Since you've also been told that the planet where these people live was colonized by settlers from Earth, why does Prime's brother seem to look like an alien? *Is* he an alien?

Well, no. He's a human being. So is Prime. But you need to understand, I think, that Prime and his brother don't look even remotely like you or me. Nobody does, up there in the far-off future.

You would have a lot of trouble, probably, believing that the human beings of that era are human beings at all. In appearance you would surely find them very *very* strange. They can put on any kind of bodily form they feel like, and they do. Some of them choose to do without bodies altogether. All of them live among miracles and wonders incomprehensible to us. The rhythm of their daily existence is nothing like ours.

Take our friend Hanosz Prime of Prime, for instance.

In his previous lifetime he had worn the popular body-modularity called "the Scimitar," which was a sleek curving design, somewhat metallic in texture and *extremely* minimalist in detail. But for this round of rejuvenation Hanosz Prime had chosen to have himself—and by *himself* what I mean is his central nervous system, his whole gestalt of brain and associated neurons and the general sensorium—installed in the modularity that was known on his planet as "the Authentic."

Authentics were aggressively virile, with great flaring shoulder-arches pivoting outward from their breastbones and a superstructure of fierce bony protrusions thrusting like a cape of quills from their upper backs. Other sharp spurs and crests of bone stood forth from the Authentic's wrists, knees, ankles, hips, and loins. You would find the general effect bizarre and frightening.

Those who had chosen this modularity invariably affected great height and mass, and bore themselves with grandiose swagger. Hanosz Prime had further underscored his intent to communicate drama and strength by adopting jet-black skin scored by scarlet slashes and an array of dangling frills of a brilliant yellow color that sprouted from his neck on all sides.

His eyes were red with yellow streaks, and their sockets were defended by three rows of bony blades.

To you, I suspect, something that looked like an Authentic would simply seem to be some kind of monster. But you'd be wrong.

All this is happening, after all, a hell of a long time from now—in the Year 777 of Cycle 888 of the 1111th Encompassment of the Ninth Mandala. I can't tell you when that year is, but it won't be arriving soon. Millions of years from now? Billions, even? Who can say? Not me. Certainly it's at least a few million years from now. Very likely a lot more.

A great deal will happen to a species' genetic map in that many years. Except for humanity—which knows how to look after itself at the expense of everybody else—and the horseshoe crab and the cockroach, which are too stubborn to evolve, all the life-forms that exist on the Earth of your time and mine will be long extinct in the Ninth Mandala. That includes cats, dogs, sheep, goats, frogs, wombats, goldfish, and anything else you might name, up to and including orangutans and chimps and gorillas. But not us. Ah, not us! We are greatly changed; but we are very much still here.

Most of the changes that have come over our species by the time of Hanosz Prime (and Sinon Kreidge and his daughter Kaivilda, and, for that matter, all the other citizens of that era) are the deliberate product of human redesign. The tinkerings of the tectogenetic microsurgeons are evident inside the body of every inhabitant of Year 777 of Cycle 888 of the 1111th Encompassment of the Ninth Mandala. Guts and gizzard, liver and lights, pancreas and spleen, ballocks and backbone—everything's been modified beyond recognition.

(Very likely you think that using long-winded designations like Year 777 of Cycle 888, etc., is a cumbersome way to keep track of time. I think so too; but you and I are not native to the Year 777 of Cycle 888 of the 1111th Encompassment of the Ninth Mandala. For those who are, the system seems simple and elegant and perfectly logical. There's no reason, really, why they should number the passage of the years the way we do, or do anything else the way we do. Besides, they're capable of communicating the entire longwinded thing, Year 777 of Cycle 888 and so forth, in a single pulse of compressed and precise meaning that to us would be nothing more than a quick flutter of sound in the upper range of audible kilohertzes.)

But—believe me—underneath all the colossal differences the people of Prime's era are still human. They are our extremely remote descendants, linked to us only by the most tenuous strands of DNA—people so far removed from us by time and evolution that we are the merest dream-fabric to them. We are phantoms out of an antiquity almost beyond comprehension to them.

All the same, try as they might, they can't fully escape from the heritage of the lumpy hairy brutish anthropoids clustered at the bottom of their family tree. They would doubt it and so would you, but even so they are our veritable kith and kin. Like us, they tick with needs and hungers and dissatisfactions, they always want more no matter how much they have, they strive endlessly to see what's over the next hill. We'd recoil in bewilderment and horror from the mere sight of them, sure; but if we could sit down and talk with them for a while we would recognize them for ourselves. They are as alien and remote from us as can be imagined; and at the same time they're just like us. In a manner of speaking.

The whole thing got arranged, with surprising ease, in short order at long range.

Hanosz Prime of Prime—young again and feeling restless, beginning his new life in startling new ways, eager to travel, suddenly desirous of seeing historic old Earth while it was still there to be seen—caused word to be sent ahead by hyperwave, using diplomatic channels, in order to get himself invited to be a house-guest at the palatial home of one of the grandest and most famous of Earth's immortal aristocrats, the distinguished and celebrated Sinon Kreidge. Even though he was—by his own choice—a former king, now, Prime still had good social connections in more than one galaxy.

And so the message went forth, pretty much instantaneously across two million light-years, through an elaborate interface of official intermediaries spanning half a dozen stellar systems, and the answer came back in a trice—a favorable one: Sinon Kreidge and Kaivilda have heard a great deal about the distinguished and celebrated Hanosz Prime of Prime, or at any rate they claim that they have, and will be happy to entertain him during his stay on Earth—and the visit was arranged.

Why not? Why not? Quick, quick, back and forth across the galaxies!

It's an age of miracles. Our own accomplishments are as nothing beside theirs, *nothing*. To the people of the Ninth Mandala, all we are is pathetic ignorant smelly primitives, mere shaggy shambling creatures from the dawn of time— despite our computers, color televisions, space satellites, and all such things.

By the time of Hanosz Prime of Prime, nine mandalas and a bunch of cycles and encompassments from now, they'll have faster-than-light starships powered by devices that don't exist even in concept right now. It'll be a simple deal to travel quickly and cheaply and easily not just between cities or continents or planets or solar systems but between whole galaxies, faster than it would be for you or me to get from New York to Kansas City. Diplomats and tourists will pop back and forth across millions of light-years in hardly any time at all, a week or two, say, from here to the quasar 3C 279, without giving it a second thought. Intergalactic messages will move even more quickly—by sub-etheric telephone, let's say, or hyperwave communicator, or some such thing.

I know, it all sounds pretty damned improbable. But stop to think a moment. We're talking about millions of years from now. The Ninth Mandala may very well be a lot farther in our future than the dinosaurs are in our past. A lot of impossible things can get to be possible in that many years.

The dinosaurs, remember, didn't know anything about anything. They were masters of the planet, but they didn't have the simplest form of technology, not a smidgeon. Hell, they couldn't even spell their own names. Look how far we've come, technologically speaking, in a mere sixty-five million years. We have computers and color television and cute little telephones and orbiting space satellites, all of them invented just a microsecond or two ago on the geological scale of things.

And for us the age of miracles is only just beginning.

En Route to Earth

So now Hanosz Prime is on his way to the threatened planet that once again calls itself Earth. Great wonders and strangenesses await him on the mother world of all humans.

His departure was uneventful. We see him now aboard his elegant little ship as it plunges Earthward at incomprehensible velocity. Manned by an invisible crew, it has swiftly made its tumble through windows and wormholes, sliding down the slippery planes, through the thin places of the cosmos, descending by sly side-passages and tricksy topological evasions across the vast reaches of the dusty intergalactic darkness. Onward it goes across the light-years (or around them, whenever possible) skimming through nebulas aglow with clotted red masses of hydrogen gas, through zones where the newest and hottest stars of the ancient universe—latecomers, lastborn of the dying galaxy, never to run their full cycle of life—valiantly hurled their fierce blue radiance into the void; and now the journey is almost over.

The small golden sun of Earth lay dead ahead. Around it danced Earth's neighboring planets, whirling tirelessly through the changeless darkness along their various orbits, filling his screens with the brilliance of their reflected light.

"Is that Earth?" he asked. "That little blue thing out there?"

"That is exactly what it is," replied the voice of Captain Tio Patcnact, who had traveled from Aldebaran to Procyon and from Procyon to Rigel in the time of the Fifth Mandala, when that was a journey worth respecting. Captain Tio Patcnact was what you would call software now, or what an earlier age than yours would probably have called a ghost; and he was in command of the small private starship in which Hanosz Prime was traveling. "It isn't all that little, either. You'll see when you get there."

"You've been there, right?"

"Quite a while ago, yes."

"But it hasn't changed much since your time, has it?"

There was a silence. Captain Tio Patcnact had never been one to speak hastily during his lifetime, and he was even less impetuous now.

"It will have changed in small details," he said, after a time. "But not in any of the large ones, I suspect. They are a fundamentally conservative people, as very wealthy people who know they are going to live forever tend to be."

Hanosz Prime of Prime considered that. He regarded himself as wealthy, as anyone who had ruled and essentially owned most of an entire planet might be thought justified in doing. But he had never considered himself fundamentally conservative. Was Captain Tio Patcnact being sarcastic, then, or patronizing, or simply rude?—or trying to prepare him for the shock of his life?

"How wealthy are they?" he asked, finally.

"They are all grand lords and ladies. Every one of them. And every one of them lives in a magnificent castle."

(Which is the same thing that Zereshk Poloi had told him; and so it must be true. And yet they are doomed, Prime thinks. The grand immortals of glittering Earth, living under the shadow of unanticipated destruction. Prime is fascinated by that idea. It seems so appropriate, somehow—so interestingly perverse. Earth, of all places, going to be sucked into some mysterious and absolutely unstoppable vacancy that has opened in the middle of nowhere! What is it like, he wonders, if you are one of those immortal ones—envied by all, the high aristocracy of the cosmos!—and you suddenly discover that you *are* going to die, immortal or not, when your part of the galaxy gets swallowed up by this hungry hole, an encompassment or three from now?)

(The truth is that the curiosity he feels about precisely this thing is one of the motives that has pulled him across two million light-years to Earth. He wants to see how the immortals are handling their death sentence. Will they flee? Can they flee? Or will they—*must* they—remain on Earth to its very last moments, and go bravely down with the ship? Hanosz Prime feels a kind of cold-blooded eagerness to watch at close range while they squirm on the hook of their unexpected fate. He knows that this isn't a nice thing to feel. But he doesn't really care. He's just been made young again, after all. The young are very seldom nice, though they can pretend to be when it seems important.)

"So it's true, the stories people tell about the Earthfolk, how rich and splendid they all are. And they're all perfect, too, aren't they?" said Hanosz Prime of Prime. "That's what I've been hearing about them forever. Everything in balance, harmonious and self-regulating. A perfect world of perfect people who never have to die unless they want to, and even then it's not necessarily permanent. Isn't that so, Tio Patcnact?"

"In a manner of speaking, yes."

"What does that mean?"

"It means that they think they are perfect, and that you may very well think so too."

"Ah," said Hanosz Prime, ex-ruler of Prime. He never knew when Captain Tio Patcnact was having some fun with him. That was one of the problems of being only a couple of centuries old, more or less, in a time when most people tended to be very long-lived indeed and certain highly privileged ones like the people of Earth were capable of living forever.

You may be wondering how it is that the name by which they call the world, up there in the Year 777 of Cycle 888 of the 1111th Encompassment of the Ninth Mandala, can be *Earth*. Yes, the selfsame Anglo-Saxon monosyllable, beginning in the back of the throat and ending with the tongue on the tips of the teeth, that we (some of us) use in our own primitive little era.

(They don't say it from the backs of their throats, though. They have no throats, not really. They do have tongues, but they're not very much like ours. They get along without teeth. But you know what I mean.)

(Or maybe you don't.)

What you want to know is, If they are so far removed from us in time—ten million years, say? Or maybe a half a billion?—how is it that they call the world by the same monosyllable that we (some of us) use today? Is it in any manner plausible that a word out of the English language of an extremely bygone era like ours should have survived into the Year 777 of Cycle 888 of the 1111th Encompassment of the Ninth Mandala?

Of course not. And in fact it didn't survive at all.

Between our time and theirs, the English language was forgotten in its entirety, just as you might suspect—along with all the other details of our civilization right down to the mere fact that it had ever existed (Shakespeare and Homer and Alexander the Great and Genghis Khan and you and me, and all our science and poetry and art and history, gone, gone, gone, lost without a trace in the strata of the eons, more thoroughly lost to them than the nickname of the australopithecus chief's brother-in-law's third wife is to us). And then all those things were rediscovered, through what we would regard as quasi-magical means, and forgotten all over again—several times, in fact. During the course of all that forgetting and remembering and re-forgetting, the third planet of that smallish yellowish sun came to be known, to its vastly altered inhabitants as well as to the inhabitants of the numerous other worlds to which humanity had spread, by all manner of newer names.

And so from time to time in the great span of years that yawns between our era and theirs the people of Earth called their world this, that, and a thousand other things, or ten thousand, a whole legion of up-to-date names that came and went with the passing of the millennia and the succession of new civilizations upon the embers and dust of older ones. And some of those new names for the planet would have seemed very strange indeed to us, mere gargles or gasps, or spurts of air, or brief blurts of brightness in the years when people spoke with colors instead of words.

But then a sleeping Seer peering into the fathomless past found the memory of the memory of the antique word buried down in the deep dream-strata where the ruins of the world you and I inhabit are destined to lie, and had brought it back to share with his friends, and they all admired the heft and measure of the ancient name and they adopted it with delight, right then and there. *Earth!* they cried. Yes! How quaint, how fine! Let's call this world of ours *Earth!* What fun! And so it was.

Brooding, Prime paces the length and breadth of the ship. That doesn't take long. It's quite a fine ship, but it isn't very big. Prime keeps it for his personal use, for jaunts between the planets of the Parasol system and occasionally to nearby star-groups. He's never taken it this far before.

Curving inlays of silver and burnished bronze brighten the walls. Heavy draperies of azure velvet flocked with gold add that little extra touch of regal splendor. Along the sides of the main cabin are holographic portraits of previous members of the royal family, twenty or thirty of them selected at random from the royal portrait gallery. Prime hadn't put them there; they came with the ship, and he had always felt it would be rude to pull them down. The most impressive portrait of the bunch is that of Prime's formidable grandfather, the fierce old undying tyrant who had finally relented and sired an heir in his six thousandth year, and then had lived another thousand anyway, so that Prime's father had had the throne hardly more than a cycle or two. The old man's deep-set eyes burn like suns: he seems ready to step down from the wall and take command of the ship.

"But even *you* had to die eventually, you old bastard," Prime says, staring at the ferocious, implacable holographic face. "You fought and kicked all the way to the end, but the end couldn't be avoided forever. Whereas the great lords and ladies of Earth—"

Prime can't stop thinking about them. Immortals who have to die! What a dirty joke the universe has played on them! What a nasty sense of irony the gods must have!

(Like most relatively young men, Prime had never given a great deal of thought to the subject of dying. It just hadn't concerned him much. Twice already he had had the experience of growing old, yes, and he hadn't cared for it at all, but he had known each time that it was only a short-term problem, with rebirth waiting just around the corner for him, and then a whole series of rebirths beyond that one for at least a couple of thousand years to come. You or I might think that speaking of someone who has already had two hundred years of life as a "relatively young man" was pretty odd, but Prime knew that he was still just at the beginning of his long span—only a green kid, as things went in the Ninth Mandala.)

(In a vague way he had supposed that he would have to die some day, since dying seemed to be the universal rule of life—except on Earth, where death had been pretty much repealed—but the end of his life was an event so far in his future that it had very little reality for him. Still, the awareness—however dim—that you are bound to die eventually, even if the time of your death is probably some thousands of years in the future, gives your life a coloration that is quite a bit different from the one that comes from knowing that you will never need to die at all.)

(The closest thing to an immortal Prime had ever known was his grandfather, whose grip on life had been so unrelentingly tenacious. But after seven thousand years even he had

had to yield finally to the facts of life as it was lived on the worlds of the Parasol system.)

(The people who lived on Earth, though, didn't have to die at all, unless they chose to, and that sort of thing wasn't exactly common. Why the Earthfolk were exempt from death was something widely discussed, and widely misunderstood, on the other inhabited worlds of the universe. The usual explanation that you would hear was that the techniques of body-flushing employed on Earth were simply more effective than those used elsewhere—that the Earthfolk had some sort of special secret method which attained absolute perfection in ridding the body of impurities. But shrewder minds then would wonder why no one from any other planet had ever managed to steal such a highly desirable secret—for no one had, and not for lack of trying. Rejuvenations using Earth techniques didn't seem to produce any unusually favorable results when tried elsewhere. So perhaps there wasn't any technical secret at all—perhaps the apparent immortality of the Earthfolk was just some inexplicable benefit that came with living on the oldest human-inhabited world in the universe. For it had been widely noticed that Earthfolk, though they did occasionally visit other planets, rarely stayed there long, invariably scuttling back to their home world after absences of no more than fifty or a hundred years.)

(And in fact that theory was pretty much the truth. It was the combination of superior technical skill—for the Earthfolk *did* have better techniques of body-flushing than anyone else, though not quite good enough to ensure eternal life—and the special environment of Earth that did the trick. The great advantage that the Earthfolk had was that they lived under the sun of Earth and breathed the air of Earth, which was something that no one else in the universe could claim. And there was something unquantifiable but potent about that unique sunlight and that unique air which—coupled with the special Earth body-flushing techniques—permitted an apparently infinite number of rebirths. At least, nobody yet had failed to emerge successfully from the rebirth tanks of Earth, even after a hundred rejuvenations, even after a thousand. But Earthfolk who spent prolonged periods on other planets—a couple of cycles, say—didn't enjoy the same immunity from mortality, even when the superior rebirth techniques of Earth were employed. After a time, they would begin to die if they did not return to their native world, which they immediately did. It was the sunlight, then; it was the air. You could live forever, if you were of the Earth. But you had to live on Earth.)

(Whenever he has thought of *them*—the wondrous Earthfolk, ageless and eternal on the great mother world— Prime has felt callow and raw by comparison. They must be like gods, he would think; and he would look toward them with the same mixture of awe and incomprehension and bitter envy that everyone had for them.)

(And so, now that they appear to be in serious peril, he wants to go among them, to experience the quality of their lives, to see how they're coping. Prime, who more or less knows that he must die some day even though he has never taken the notion very seriously, wants to see how people who had thought they were entirely exempt from that fate are dealing with the knowledge that they aren't. For all he knows, he might even have something to give them. For there is real tragedy there; and in the rashness and arrogance of his restored youth Prime intends, if he can, to let them perceive some sense of his consciousness of his own mortality, so that they can come to terms, perhaps, with their own. Now that it has been thrust upon them like this—like a mud pie in the face.)

A Little More Essential Information

(It's probably a useful idea to point out before we go much further that the thing that is threatening the continued well-being of Earth is known as a Twisselman hypersingularity. A Twisselman hypersingularity is something very much like a black hole, but considerably more aggressive and therefore even nastier. It is formed by a gravitational collapse so intense that a perpetually widening feeder-vortex is created, a whirlpool effect hungrily sucking in adjacent space—an imperialist black hole, so to speak, driven by an unending need to expand its territory.)

(You back there in our own era don't know about Twisselman hypersingularities just yet, because Hal Twisselman is only nine years old at the moment and is currently struggling to get the hang of quadratic equations, which is pretty good going for a nine-year-old but a long way from the profound work he will eventually do. The citizens of Earth in the Ninth Mandala haven't heard of Twisselman either, because, as you are aware, he and the whole civilization that produced him dropped into historical oblivion half a dozen geological epochs before their time. But that doesn't mean that the Twisselman hypersingularity doesn't exist, only that we don't yet know its name and the Ninth Mandala folk have forgotten it. The thing itself is out there in the Milky Way gobbling away at this very moment, even so, and its insatiable appetite is gradually but steadily gaining force. Space in its vicinity is relentlessly contracting; things unlucky enough to be within range of its pull are rushing toward each other as the dark mouth gapes ever larger; and distant observers will gradually be able to detect the spectral lines of the stars in the affected region beginning to creep minutely toward the blue, indicating that they are getting closer together. The sky quite literally is falling—one little piece at a time. But everything, eventually, will drop into the Center of Things, which is the hypersingularity. It's not a good situation. It will get much worse.)

Prime activated Captain Tio Patcnact again.

"If the Earthfolk are the perfect creatures that you say they are, and immortal besides," Prime said, "what I want to ask you is, how do you think they feel about having learned that they're going to die when the stars fall into the Center of Things? Are they furious? Depressed? Trying desperately to find a way out of their trouble? — Assuming that they believe it's going to happen at all, of course. What I'm saying, Tio Patcnact, is: are they so calm and perfect and godlike that the thought of their planet's being gobbled up by some kind of black hole doesn't bother them at all? Or is it driving them out of their minds?"

"Wouldn't it bother you?" asked the captain. And then he said, "But you might be able to help them, of course."

"Help them? How?"

"They have a legend, you know. Of a king who has no kingdom, who comes to them from a far-off land at a time of great crisis, and takes their anguish upon his own shoulders, and saves them from the doom that is rushing toward them. Could that not be you? Are you not a king without a kingdom, going to them at a time of crisis from a far-off land."

"I suppose," said Hanosz Prime, pondering. A strangely chilling thought crossed his mind just then. There had also been a prophecy on Prime's own world that a member of the Prime family would meet his end at the beginning of time, but that he would emerge with godlike nature. Prime had never taken any of that seriously. It seemed pure nonsense to him. But that nonsense, and now *this* nonsense—"In a manner of speaking, yes, you could say that that is what I am. But how could I possibly save them from anything? Especially something like the end of the universe, Tio Patcnact?"

"How could you, indeed?" said Tio Patcnact, and vanished into silence.

Prime didn't like being brushed off that way, but there wasn't much he could do about it. His conversations with his crew were never very satisfying, and he hadn't found any solution for that. There was no effective way he could order his software around, except insofar as the specific functioning of the ship was concerned: they did as they pleased, otherwise. All too often the members of the crew behaved as though he were some irritating organic infestation that interfered with the orderly performance of their labors. Prime let the subject drop.

Standing by the screen, he watched the little blue globe of Earth grow rapidly larger and larger. The shapes of the continents were visible now, great wedge-shaped chunks of deckle-edged brownness arranged like the spokes of a fan in the middle of an immense sea. At sparse intervals bright spots of heat and light rose from them, glaring out of the infrared, the spectral fingerprint of the fires of life: emanations of the settled areas, the magnificent castles of the grand and immortal Earthfolk. They are few in number, so Zereshk Poloi has said, and lead lives of high and lordly privilege. Earth's total population, Prime knows, is so small as to be practically trivial: a mere few hundred thousand people, so he has heard. (At least that's the number of flesh-and-blood human beings. There are millions or even billions of simulacra and residuals and virtuals and other non-living subsidiary forms to do the dirty work of keeping civilization going.) It seems all very different from any world Prime has ever visited.

But it *should* be different, Prime told himself. This world is Earth, after all.

Earth!

Prime felt a flicker of awe, a shiver of something close to fear. He caught his breath and clenched his fists.

The eternal mother of us all!—the ancestral world—the home of civilization for billions of years, layer upon layer of epochs going back through all nine mandalas and the disorganized forgotten eras that had preceded them.

He stared at the approaching planet. Crazily, he hungered to swallow the entire thing whole, though he knew that he would not be able to manage even the smallest bite. There was a sharp pressure at his throat, a crushing heaviness in his chest, a throbbing in his skull.

An encapsulated pulse of Earth's enormous history came squirting out of his midbrain to bedazzle the outer lobes of his whirling mind. In the early hours of the voyage he had summoned from his ship's data banks all that was known about Earth; now he struggled desperately to embrace the totality of that dizzying blurt, the knowledge of all those different races and civilizations and cultures and empires of mankind, rising up and falling down and being replaced by others that in turn would disappear, wave after wave of endlessly changing but still somehow identifiably human forms over uncountable spans of time that the ship's mind had hurled into his, the Originals and the Basics and the Radiants and Serenities, the Masks and the Spinners and the Sorcerers and the Thrones, the Wanderers replacing the Star-Scriers and the Moon-Sweepers driving out the Wanderers and the Hive Folk overwhelming the Moon-Sweepers, and on and on and on, eon after eon, a great continuity of change, the whole thing forming the mountainous and incomprehensible agglomeration that was the turbulent history of the mother world. Most of which had been lost: the great mass of fact that remained, names and dates and eras and annals, was only a tiny fragment of the whole, Hanosz Prime knew, only a snippet, only a slice, a faint film with most of the substance behind it gone.

But Prime had never expected the impact to be as strong as this.

He could barely handle it all. He was stunned, staggered, overwhelmed by the proximity of this ancientmost planet of the human realm, standing as it was atop the throne of its own gigantic past.

"Help me," he murmured. "I'm overloading. The whole weight of human history is falling on me. I'm choking under it."

The ship's medic—Farfalla Vlinder was his name, a native of Boris in the Borboleta system, still a resident there at that moment, as a matter of fact, but duplicated under contract for use in starships—said quickly, "Don't try to take in all of Earth, its whole outrageous past and present, in a single gulp. No one can absorb all that. There's too much, much too much."

"Yes—but—"

"Think of now and nothing but now. Think just of a single district, a single town, a single house. Think of Sinon Kreidge's great palace. And think of his daughter Kaivilda. Especially Kaivilda. Focus on her. How beautiful she is. How eager you are to see her."

"Yes. Yes."

(The medic has the right idea. Limit your perspective, control your ruminations.)

Yes. Prime will allow himself to think only of Kaivilda.

Of course he has no idea at this point what she looks like, other than that she is beautiful. Prime has seen her often enough in dreams as his scrying mind crossed the galaxies, but that was only in dreams. Her true shape is unknown to him; in his dreams she is formless, nothing more than a golden aura stippled with amethyst and bright ruby. Her colors and textures call to him across the endless night of space.

Of the real Kaivilda, though, Prime knows almost nothing. All he has to work with are the fragmentary things Zereshk Poloi had said concerning Sinon Kreidge and his splendid daughter, details which had aroused his curiosity concerning the former and somewhat different feelings toward the latter. Zereshk Poloi had spoken of Kaivilda's seraphic elegance, her luminous intelligence, her wondrous tranquility of spirit, above all her extraordinary beauty. But Zereshk Poloi had couched it all in the most general way, foggy raptures short on specific detail; and Prime had not been interested enough, then, to ask for amplification. Now he is; but now Zereshk Poloi is off on his travels again, no one knows where.

So Prime does the best he can. He summons up an ideal construct of Beauty, telling himself that it represents Kaivilda, and concentrates on that. A column of pure music shimmers in his mind. The lines of the full spectrum pulsate at its core. Umbrellas of cool light descend upon him.

And it works. The imagined image of Kaivilda that he has conjured up for himself steadies him. The massive burden of Earth is lifted from him. Prime no longer feels pinned under the vast weight of the eons.

"Shall we begin landing procedures?" asks Captain Tio Patcnact.

"Begin them, yes. Immediately."

The screen brightens. Earth rushes forward until it seems that the whole planet is leaping into his hands.

The tiny scarlet teardrop that is his starship arches across the orbit of ponderous swirling Hjentiflir, which you would call Jupiter, and plunges past the great flower-shaped pattern of eternally blazing matter which the Star-Scrier people of the 104th Encompassment had fabricated for their amusement and pleasure from the otherwise useless clutter which we know as the asteroid belt, and swoops toward the landing stage of Sinon Kreidge's Keep on the eastern coast of Earth's great central continent.

Hanosz Prime steps from his ship. And instantly he sees that Zereshk Poloi did not lie to him. This is indeed a planet of wonders and miracles.

Golden sunlight runs in rivers across the iron-blue sky, dazzling him.

Stars shine at midday in the firmament.

It is warm here, even on this mountaintop, much warmer than on snowy Prime. The sweet unfamiliar air of Earth, thin but not harsh, sweeps about him and as he sucks it in it seems to him that he is drinking down the mellowed wine of antiquity, thousands of cycles old.

There is magic in that strange air. Ancient sorceries, floating dissolved in the fragrant atmosphere like flecks of gold in a rare elixir, penetrate his being.

Prime looks around, numbed, dazed. A figure materializes out of the shimmering haze and gestures to him.

It is Kaivilda. She has been waiting at the rim of the landing stage to greet him when he arrives; and now she moves toward him with heartrending grace, as though she is drifting weightless through the strange thin air.

SINON KREIDGE AND HIS DAUGHTER

PRIME HAS REACHED KALAHIDE KEEP on the black, craggy basalt summit of Mount Vorn above the Oracle Plain: the highest point of one of Earth's loftiest mountains. That is the home of Sinon Kreidge, who has chosen to deploy himself in the Original modularity, and therefore believes that he is essentially indistinguishable in physical form from you or me.

(He's wrong about that, but he'll never know it.)

What of Sinon Kreidge himself? Who is he? What manner of man?

A complex and sophisticated individual, wealthy and powerful and shrewd; a personage of grandeur and significance. Everyone would agree to that. Perceptive, influential, considerate, domineering, ruthless—all those terms would apply. And, of course, mutable, very much so.

In his present matrix-construct Sinon Kreidge of Earth has preferred to present himself as stern, dour, a somber crystalline spirit permeated through and through by a pervasive melancholy. In previous matrices of recent memory he had been in turn boisterous, lascivious, vagrant, parsimonious, insistently generous, and untiringly witty. He plans to be scholarly and withdrawn, a dry cloistered soul, in his next. His far-ranging memory can travel back over thousands of years, scores of matrices, whole constellations of lives within the infinity that is his life.

Like everybody else, on Earth and elsewhere, Sinon Kreidge is fond of changing not only his personality-matrix but his modularity—his outward physical appearance—every once in a while. His most recent change of modularity took place just a short while before Hanosz Prime's arrival on Earth. Very suddenly—right around the time that everyone he knew had begun talking about the possibility that the Earth was going to be destroyed—Kreidge had grown weary of his current modularity, the Radiant (jagged bolts of light, medallions of brilliant metal) and had decided to have himself turned into an Original.

What attracted him to that modularity was the idea that it was believed to be a close imitation of the ancestral form of latter-day humanity, the form that flourished in the last epoch before widespread genetic manipulation became commonplace. If the world was going to end, Sinon Kreidge thought, then he might as well look like something out of its dawn. There was a nice poetic circularity in that.

But, of course, nobody in the Ninth Mandala had much of an idea what we people of the world's dawn actually looked like. They had nothing to go by but guesswork, and the guess wasn't particularly accurate.

The new Original-modularity Sinon Kreidge, in fact, would look to us more like an ape than like any person of what we like to call modern times. His chest was immensely deep and broad, his arms dangled almost to the ground, his brows were great simian ridges forming shadowed caverns for his eyes, his body was entirely covered with coarse red hair down to and including the soles of his feet. It's not at all flattering to us, really. You would realize at once if you saw him that the Seers, reaching backward through time via the medium of dreams to recapture snatches of our impossibly prehistoric era, had fallen victim to some false assumptions about exactly how primordial we were. And you'd probably be a little irked.

You need to consider, though, that from the vantage point of Ninth Mandala times, the first few million years of human evolution are all jumbled together in a blur. They don't realize that we regard Pithecanthropus erectus and the Neanderthal man as very different in physical appearance from ourselves. To them, we're all a bunch of hairy farting apes.

But it isn't quite as bad as all that. There are many characteristics of the Original modularity that do indicate that Sinon Kreidge in his present configuration is considerably more than an ape. He holds himself magnificently upright, an almost godlike posture, and his limbs, though oddly proportioned, are finely formed; his facial expression is alert and inquisitive beneath those beetling brows; his movements are agile and swift. He smiles easily and reveals what could almost be teeth, white and flawless. His forehead is an imposing rounded vault, not at all primitive, and there is obviously a capable brain behind it, in fact a supremely intelligent one. What he would seem to us to be, in fact, is a splendid if somewhat curiously formed man of ancient times, a man of unusual grandeur of bearing and obvious physical strength, who for some unfortunate reason is strangely bestial in appearance. We would think of him as part demigod and part ape, but probably more demigod than ape. The people of the 1111th of the Ninth may very likely think of us the other way around, if they think of us at all. They may not even be aware that civilized human life had existed on Earth as far back in geological antiquity as the period which we of the early twenty-first century call "the twenty-first century."

As Prime approaches Earth, Sinon Kreidge finds himself in a very bad mood.

The recent bleak cosmological news has had a heavy impact on Sinon Kreidge's spirits, which in his current matrix had been somber enough to begin with. Like everyone else on Earth since immortality became an established fact there, Kreidge has always assumed that an endless life of infinite and unlimited possibilities lay before him. Now he is being told that the entire galaxy in which he resides is imperiled, in fact may soon be reaching its culminating moment and is destined to disappear into the maw of a voracious astronomical anomaly which has been eating its way toward Earth since the beginning of time. The way things look, he has two choices: he can stay on Earth and die, or he can leave his native planet's unique protective zone—and die.

That news has made Sinon Kreidge exceedingly pensive.

In fact he is—let's not put too fine a point on it—in real agony. He's engulfed in dark despair.

That's a new emotion for Sinon Kreidge, despair. He's never felt anything like it. His long life has been all triumph, glory, splendor—up till now; but now he aches with the bitter awareness that the unavoidable End of All is rushing toward him, and not only him, but toward everyone, everyone. Infinite power and immeasurable glory and actual physical immortality—complete access, in short, to all the well-nigh miraculous wonders of the age he is lucky enough to live in—don't mean a damn when the fabric of space seems to be collapsing, when the whole galaxy and for all anyone knows the entire universe itself is shortly going to fold up into something small enough to lose inside a microbe. There's no room for a catastrophe like that in Sinon Kreidge's philosophy; he has no experience with such things as frustration and disappointment, let alone complete futility and helplessness, and he doesn't know what to make of them, how to assimilate them and come to some acceptance of them. Life hasn't prepared him for the possibility of disaster on this scale.

He tries to find ways to deal with it.

At first he tells himself—and others, sometimes—that he finds the possibility of disaster absolutely fascinating. It is so long since he has felt a new emotion of any sort that he actually revels in the novelty of the death sentence that has apparently fallen upon his world. He will wear black and affect a pale, brooding demeanor. He will play sad music. He will arrange for rain to fall frequently in the vicinity of his castle.

It almost does the trick. But in fact he is haunted constantly now by his fate and the subterfuges can't fully help him shake it off. Contemplation of the coming disaster dims his every moment. Such dark feelings are novel to Sinon Kreidge, and very disagreeable. Sinon Kreidge tries to keep his brooding to himself, however, and mainly he succeeds.

Mainly.

And as for the lovely Kaivilda:

It wasn't usual, on Earth in Ninth Mandala days, for people to have children. A planet where in the ordinary course of things nobody died was not a place where people felt much need for reproducing. But Sinon Kreidge had always been a little unusual. So he had formed a sleek and supple daughter out of a handful of dust while he was in one of his previous matrices, thinking he would keep her for a matrix or two and eventually dissolve her when he entered into some new identity in which having a daughter might be inconvenient.

But she was a pleasing companion and Sinon Kreidge had decided, a couple of matrix transformations later, to allow her a permanent existence. Kaivilda was grateful to him for that, but her gratitude was mingled with the acrid knowledge that he might at any time have deprived her of life without a thought, just as casually as he had given it to her. She took pains to be cordial with him at every moment, however. She knew he could easily reverse himself—arbitrarily, no reason at all required—and send her from the world. He had the right. And in his present bleak mood he might do almost anything. She had been his unilateral creation, after all. His power over her was total. No treaties or bonds had been posted at the time of her making. "Let Kaivilda be," Sinon Kreidge had said, and so she was. To bring a child at all into this era was unusual; to retain it on a permanent basis was quite extraordinary, though of course that did happen now and then. On the other hand, Kaivilda thinks, if we're all going to die, what difference does it make to me whether it happens sooner or later? And then she thinks, On the third hand, I'd rather have it be later. Much later.

And A Look at Their Castle

How CAN ONE DESCRIBE Kalahide Keep, the ancestral home of Prime's soon-to-be host, Sinon Kreidge?

Here's a pack of adjectives for you:

Extraordinary.

Magnificent.

Extravagant.

Luxurious.

Resplendent.

Fine grandiloquent words, and all of them accurate enough as far as they go. No one in any era, scrutinizing Sinon Kreidge's splendid castle on the precarious tip of dark and shining Mount Vorn, would quarrel with the use of *magnificent* and *luxurious* and *resplendent*. But *extravagant*? Not really, not when you consider that Sinon Kreidge's means are essentially infinite, and therefore inexhaustible. How can someone of inexhaustible means be extravagant? And *extraordinary*? In comparison to what? Everyone who lives on the world that has decided to call itself Earth again lives in a dwelling that most people of earlier eras would have considered extraordinary. *Everyone.* If the entire population of a world (although it is not a very large population) lives in some sort of magnificent, luxurious, and resplendent dwelling, what then does *extraordinary* mean? To live in a mud hut, in the year 777 of Cycle 888, would have been extraordinary. Or an igloo, a tent, a thatched cottage. But a castle? In the context of the epoch of Sinon Kreidge and his contemporaries, a castle is quite an ordinary thing. Everyone has one. Earth's population is quite small and there's no reason not to live graciously. Earlier people would often say that one's home is one's castle; in the year 777 of Cycle 888 the terms of the equation are reversed: one's castle is merely one's dwelling, one's residence, one's home. No two are alike; but all of them are magnificent, luxurious, resplendent. We may as well concede extravagant and extraordinary as well.

Sinon Kreidge's dwelling—which, I hope you realize now, was quite ordinary in its extraordinary way—was organic in nature, a living, growing thing, and therefore it had gone through a host of changes during the eleven generations of its occupation by members of the Kalahide family, to which Sinon Kreidge belonged. In its present configuration it had the look of a vast and gleaming onyx serpent, looping and leaping along the knifeblade-sharp ridge of metal that is Mount Vorn's highest peak.

The uppermost of its many levels, a transparent bubble of clearest quartz, contained Sinon Kreidge's private bedchamber, with his conjuratorium just alongside. Below that—a horn-like excrescence of pure shining platinum boldly cantilevered out over the valley—was his trophy room and the chamber of his ancestral shrines; and just beside that, a blatant green eye of curving emerald, was the jutting hemisphere of his harmonic retreat.

A long white-vaulted passageway led at a steeply descending angle to the isolated apartments of Sinon Kreidge's graceful daughter Kaivilda. Access to these was guarded by a row of slender but effective blades, keen as razors, that would rise from the carnelian slabs of the passageway floor at the slightest provocation: the footfall of a mouse, let us say. (Earth has its perils, even in the Ninth Mandala.) A cascading series of balconies gave Kaivilda access to the fresh mountain air and the always stimulating view of the Plain of Oracles, where swarms of virtual realities cluster and hive.

A second passageway in the opposite direction opened into an elaborate pleasure-gallery supported by pillars of golden marble. Here the inhabitants of the Keep could swim in a shimmering pool lined with garnet slabs, or suspend themselves in a column of warm air and permit streams of unquantified sensation to flood their sensoria, or put themselves in contact—through appropriate connectors and conduits—with the rhythms and sighing pulses of the cosmos. Here, also, Sinon Kreidge maintained patterned rugs for focused meditation, banks of motile light-organisms for autohypnosis, a collection of stimulatory pistons and cartridges, and other useful devices.

From here the structure made an undulating swaybacked curve and sent two wings back up the mountain at differing levels. One contained Sinon Kreidge's collection of zoological marvels, the other his botanical garden. Between them, dangling in breathtaking verticality, were two levels of libraries and chambers for the housing of antiquities, bric-a-brac, and miscellaneous objets d'art. Centrally positioned between these rooms the castle's grand dining hall was appended, a single sturdy octagonal block of polished agate thrusting far out into the abyss.

The next level downward, the lowest of the series, was the room of social encounter, a cavernous hall where Sinon Kreidge entertained the many guests, mainly Earthborn but occasionally from other worlds, that so frequently accepted his hospitality; appropriately lavish accommodations for those guests were located nearby. A landing stage for the convenience of these visitors' vehicles protruded from the mountain alongside. Behind it, hewn deep into the face of the mountain, were kitchens, waste-removal facilities, power-generation chambers, servants' quarters, and all the myriad other utilitarian rooms that served the castle's needs.

Five thousand years earlier, the building had had an entirely different form. It had been a squat black polyhedral fortress then, a sparse cluster of huge airy rooms of stark and even brutal simplicity, protected by immense buttressed walls. Its style had been widely admired and even imitated, which perhaps was why Sinon Kreidge had abruptly ordered it to transform itself to something totally other.

And five thousand years hence it would look like—well, who could say? Something just as different, no doubt. Sinon Kreidge was a mutable man. Change (within reasonable limits, of course) had always given him much delight. Surely he would tire of his castle's present magnificence, luxury, and splendor somewhere in the next five thousand years. The next time around, he may want a mud hut. Or an igloo.

Assuming there is a next time.

Something anomalous is chewing up the continuum in the back reaches of Earth's galaxy, don't forget, and it doesn't want to stop. As Sinon Kreidge is only too aware, it's swallowing everything there is, treating itself to an unhurried but totally unsparing feast—not just putting away the soup and the fish course and the roast loin of pork, but eating the dishes, silverware, table and chair as well, and the rest of the dining-room furniture, and then starting in on the house and grounds and garden. And Earth is getting closer and closer to that insatiable gnawing mouth all the time.

First Impressions:
The Arrival at the Keep

To his great relief Hanosz Prime, stepping from his ship into the warm alien air of Earth, was instantly struck by the perfection of Kaivilda's beauty. It's the good old *click!* we all know so well, still operating up there in the remote Ninth Mandala. For him, for her. *Click!* Ninth Mandala love is nothing very much like love as we understand the term, nor is sex, as you'll see, nor is marriage. But the *click!*—the good old pheromonal *click!*—that hasn't changed at all.

Prime had known a little of what to expect, but Kaivilda goes far beyond anything he had imagined from the advance reports. His informants have not lied to him, Prime sees now, not in any way. She is wondrous—flawless—superb. She inspires in him, immediately, dreams of the activity that *they* up there in the Ninth Mandala call "rapport" and that you can't really understand at all, rapport being the Ninth Mandala equivalent of love and sex and quite a good deal more besides. And Kaivilda is equally charmed by Hanosz Prime. The mere sight of him has set her glowing all up and down the spectrum.

Young love! At first sight, no less! In any era, it's something to admire and envy.

(But what an odd pair our young couple would seem to us to be! For them it's love at first sight—sheer physical attraction. You, on the other hand, would probably find her exceedingly weird-looking and not in the least attractive, and him terrifying and downright repellent.)

You already know that Hanosz Prime had had himself done up as an Authentic, awesome and swaggering and virile, for his newest identity-matrix. As for Kaivilda, she had lately adopted the modularity known as the Serenity, which had come into fashion only recently. Like most of the modularities that were popular in this decadent age it was of an antiquarian nature: a resurrection of one of the many vanished forms through which the human species had passed in the course of its long voyage through time. The original Serenities, a long-vanished human species that had been dominant in the peaceful and cultivated period known as the Fifth Mandala, had been oval in form, tender and vulnerable in texture: tapering custardy masses of taut cream-hued flesh equipped with slender supporting limbs and ornamented along their upper surfaces with a row of unblinking violet eyes of the keenest penetration. The motions of a Serenity were heart-breakingly subtle, a kind of vagrant drifting movement that had the quality of a highly formal antique dance. All this had been quite accurately reproduced in the modern recreation.

So neither Prime nor Kaivilda would appear to be in any way human to you, nor did either one look remotely like the other. But why should they? For one thing, there's been all that time for evolutionary change to take place (not to mention a lot of deliberate genetic fiddling-around for cosmetic purposes) in the thousands of centuries that separate their time from ours. In the Ninth Mandala—when the various races of humanity were spread across billions of worlds and millions of light-years, and just about anything was technologically possible—you could, as we've already noted, take on any physical form you cared to; or none at all, for that matter. (The disembodied form—for those who liked to travel light—was still a minority taste, but not really rare.) No reasons existed for everyone to look like everyone else. Everybody understood this. Nobody was troubled by it.

To you, then, Kaivilda would seem like a gigantic boiled egg, peeled of its shell, adorned with a row of blue eyes and a slit of a mouth and a few other external features like arms and a pair of spindly legs.

It would be hard for you to find much physical appeal in that, I suspect. No matter how kinky you like to think you are, Kaivilda just wouldn't be your type.

But you aren't Hanosz Prime of Prime, and this isn't the 1111th Encompassment of the Ninth Mandala. Your tastes aren't relevant to what turns Prime on, and vice versa. So maybe you'd be better off to forget what I've just told you about what she looks like. If you're a man, you'll have a lot simpler time of it if you try to see her as your own ideal of present-day feminine beauty, whatever that may be—a tall willowy blonde or a petite brunette or a voluptuous redhead, whatever kind of woman turns you on the most. And if you're female you may find that it will also help to forget all I said about Hanosz Prime's oppressive bulk and mass, the sharp bony quills jutting from his upper back, the other lethal-looking spurs and crests of bone sticking out elsewhere on his body, and those fleshy yellow frills dangling from his neck. Think of him as a lanky, good-looking young guy of about twenty-five who went to a nice Ivy League school, wears expensive sweaters, and drives a neat little Mercedes-Benz sports car.

(I suppose you may argue that that would be cheating. Okay: go ahead, then, and get yourself into a proper Ninth Mandala mind-set. Hanosz Prime looks like a cross between a compact two-legged dinosaur and a small battle-tank, and Kaivilda like a giant boiled egg mounted on a pair of very spindly legs. And each one thinks right away that the other is tremendously sexy, as that concept is understood in Ninth Mandala times, though I assure you that sex as we understand it is definitely not a custom of the era. There you are. Cope with it any way you can.)

As Prime stood frozen and gaping with delight and awe, Kaivilda moved smoothly to his side and said, speaking softly with her fingertips, "Welcome to Kalahide Keep, Hanosz Prime."

"How beautiful it is to be here," said Hanosz Prime. It was an effort for him to frame words at first, but he managed. "What a marvelous house. And what a glorious planet this is. How delighted I am to look upon its ancient hills and valleys."

(Meaning: *How pleased I am to be near you. How satisfactory a being you seem to be. What a splendid challenge you are.* Both of them understood this.)

"Come," Kaivilda said. She took him by one of his bony wrist-spurs and gently drew him into the Keep. "You will have to meet my father first, of course. We've heard so much about you; he's eager to meet you. And then: Would you care to air-swim? Shall we feed? What about a tour of our Third Mandala ruins?

"Everything," said Hanosz Prime. "Everything at once. My appetites are extreme."

"My father, first," said Kaivilda.

(They've heard so much about me, Prime thinks. What can they have heard? And from whom?) The universe is full of worlds. What can they know about distant Prime and its youthful king? He decides that they're merely being polite, in their aristocratic Earth way, to the provincial visitor from the unimportant planet in the Parasol system—wherever that may be; how would they know; why would they care?—of the Andromeda Galaxy.

Kaivilda led him deeper within the castle. Meanwhile several servants of the Keep, reconstituting themselves from the plasmatic residual state known as *equipoise* in which they stored themselves when not needed, fell upon his ship and swept it into an equally temporary dissolution, crew and all.

Prime covertly studied Kaivilda out of the corner of the corner of his eye. And, he was quite sure, she was studying him the same way. Little auras of mutual delight circled in the air above them. Dancing pheromones traveled giddily back and forth between them. Something of a romantic nature was already cooking: definitely cooking.

(You might immediately object that any attempt by an Authentic like Prime, prickly and fierce-textured, to embrace the quivering tremulous flesh of a soft-bodied Serenity like Kaivilda would surely end in disaster. You would very likely be right. But Hanosz Prime's dream of achieving rapport with Kaivilda included nothing so gross and crude as direct physical contact of that sort, I assure you.)

Kaivilda took Prime through vaulted corridors and great echoing spaces into the vastness of the room of social encounter. Sinon Kreidge emerged now from one of the inner chambers of Kalahide Keep to present himself. His expression was crisp, almost frosty, showing the severity of which Prime had been warned. Kreidge greeted his guest with outstretched arms and a searching smile that quickly faded to a carefully controlled austerity of manner. Evidently Kreidge meant to be friendly but not *too* friendly.

Prime was struck immediately by the grandeur and puissance of Sinon Kreidge's presence: a man of great authority, a man of superb self-assurance.

Though Kreidge in his recently adopted Original modularity glows with raw physical vigor, there is an aura of great age about him, too. In that sense he reminds Prime of his late unlamented grandfather, but he senses that Kreidge may be even older. Kreidge could well be twenty thousand years old, or fifty thousand, or a million. There's no way of telling. Prime has a sense of an infinity of selves superimposed here, one upon another like archaeological strata. He feels dwarfed by Sinon Kreidge's evident store of accumulated life-experience; he feels like a child—no, like less than a child, like something only half-born—beside him.

But there is something deeply contradictory about the formidable Sinon Kreidge, Prime realizes in the next moment. Kreidge has arrived, surprisingly, accompanied by a cloud of somber dissonant music that almost immediately seems to signal to Hanosz Prime the presence of some sort of keen distress in the private places of his host's soul. It is there for only an instant, and then it is gone, disappearing so quickly that Prime wonders whether he had actually perceived anything at all. But no; no. The dissonance had really been there. Prime is certain of that. For that one instant, Prime knows, he has seen right through Sinon Kreidge's outer mask into the hidden agony at the core of the great lord's innermost being.

So it is just as Prime has suspected. The situation of these Earthfolk, now that they have found out that they must die just like everyone else, is grim. Kreidge appears to be despondent beneath the weight of that knowledge. And with good reason.

Consider: All the fierce effort of the ages, mandala after long mandala of dedicated progress toward the attainment of perfection here on Earth, has led, finally, to nothing more than a crushing irony, a feeble foolish joke. The climax of humanity's long existence is apparently going to be a terrible and inescapable tragedy—out, out, all striving a waste, everything destined to be snuffed like a candle!—and Sinon Kreidge is caught up in that tragedy without recourse or hope; and this has stained his soul with a blackness that can never be expunged.

(Hanosz Prime feels an instant surge of something very close to glee. It's embarrassing, but he can't help it: he's human, isn't he? *Schadenfreude!* Joy in the misfortunes of others! What greater misfortune could there be than the destruction of a world exempt from death? What greater joy than a mortal's contemplation of the pain of these immortals who know now that they would, after all, have to die?)

Sinon Kreidge is a man in great pain, then. Prime is sure of that now. Prime may be very young as youthfulness is reckoned in his era, but he's neither naive nor unintelligent.

As though aware that Prime had guessed his secret and eager to retreat behind a wall of distraction, the master of Kalahide Keep offered some further token of greeting—a quick conjuring-display, a commanding barrage of colors and sounds and sights that ricocheted awesomely from the angular blocks of chalcedony that formed the walls of the imposing chamber.

Hanosz Prime—young, yes, but well-bred, a true gentleman—avoided making the commonplace response, an attempt at equal or perhaps superior sensory effects. That would have been offensive as well as foolhardy. Instead he performed a sweeping gesture of obeisance and imposed on himself a total change of body color from the violent and melodramatic blacks and yellows and scarlets that he preferred to more submissive pastels.

These colors he held until Sinon Kreidge, by his smile and relaxed stance, indicated that he was pleased; then the visitor, in some relief, resumed his former ferocious tonality.

***

(Preliminary social gestures are necessary, now. Sinon Kreidge asks Hanosz Prime whether his voyage has been a pleasant one. It was most uneventful, says Hanosz Prime, but quite agreeable all the same. Sinon Kreidge makes the appropriate expressions of gratitude for that. He offers other properly hospitable pieties. He does seem to know a little about Prime's home world, after all. He even asks whether Prime has left his brother as regent. So apparently some research has been done. Prime is surprised by that, and flattered.)

(Everything about Kreidge is quite formal in manner and his voice is melodious and well modulated. Sinon Kreidge appears to be utterly in command of himself now. But there is a lingering coloration to his tone that hearkens back to that earlier moment of revelation. Hanosz Prime has no doubt now that he is seeing within Sinon Kreidge the clearly perceptible presence of a certain deep and intense pool of melancholy, not quite completely concealed behind the elegant facade of that lordly persona, which can only be a response to—what else could matter to such a man?—the coming death of the universe. A dark and tangible bitterness streams from that hidden place like the heavy light of a black sun.)

(I would comfort him if I could, Hanosz Prime thinks. But what help can there possibly be for something like this?)

THE ANGUISH OF SINON KREIDGE

"WELL," SINON KREIDGE SAID, GESTURING to the gleaming wall of crystal rising steeply in front them. "You see all of Earth spread out before you. Please treat it as your own to use as you wish, so long as you are with us."

"It *is* my own, sir," Prime replied smoothly. "For which one of us, throughout the universe, is not ultimately a king of Earth?"

"Indeed. Indeed. Nicely put," said Sinon Kreidge. And he exchanged glances with Kaivilda, as though they were admiring his swiftness with a compliment.

You have become a very glib bastard indeed in this new matrix of yours, Prime tells himself.

"Shall I explain to you what the things are that you see out there below us?" asked Kaivilda in the softest of tones.

"If you would," said Prime. "Please."

They approached the great crystal wall.

"Directly below the Keep," she said, "we have the Oracle Plain. In its shapes and colors are the answers to all the questions that have ever been asked and many that have not yet been framed. You will want to visit it, I think, but not immediately: it could create troublesome disturbances of the soul for you, and it may be too soon after your voyage to take that risk. Beyond the Plain, to the left, is Lake Serifice. Those mountains over there are called the Angelons: they are studded everywhere on their surface with fabulous gems. You walk on a carpet of rubies and emeralds. A wizard condensed them out of weeds and trash in the Sixth Mandala; we have had no regard for such jewels ever since. Further on—almost at the horizon—you may see a body of motionless black water. That's the Sea of Miaule, with Sapont Island smoldering just off shore. The island has been on fire as far back as anyone knows. It's a place of demons and basilisks: I'll take you to see them, if you're curious."

"And that dismal mound of gray rubble closer to us, there in the middle distance?"

"The ruined city of Costa Stambool, which flourished in the Third Mandala and was totally destroyed at the outset of the violent Fourth. We've rebuilt it here as a pleasure park."

"Rebuilt it in the form of a ruin?" asked Hanosz Prime, in surprise.

"Precisely. It seemed more beautiful that way. Simply reconstructing it as it looked when it was first built would have been much too obvious."

Hanosz Prime pondered that. Why not? he thought? "Yes. I think I take your meaning."

"The dark triangular object just at the limit of vision," continued Kaivilda, "is the mountain of High Grambodge, with

Megalila Keep at its summit. That's the residence of our closest neighbors, Rufiel Kisimir and Lady Heiss Vaneille. We'll visit them later, if you like, though sometimes they can be unfriendly."

Sinon Kreidge said, "Or stupid. Rufiel Kisimir is a Quietist with Handdara pretensions; Lady Heiss Vaneille is of the opposite persuasion, an extreme Activist, a very embarrassing one."

"Father—" Kaivilda said, sounding distinctly uneasy. "You know that you'll only upset yourself if—"

Sinon Kreidge held up one hand to silence her. His fingers were very slender, with fingernails like long jeweled talons. The hand itself was trembling perceptibly. Kreidge's interior turmoil seemed to have risen to the surface once again and this time he was making scarcely any attempt to hide it. It was like the breaking of a dam: everything that was held in check within him was plainly about to come rushing uncontrollably forth.

To Hanosz Prime he said, in a voice thick with emotion (not really a voice, not thick as we understand thick; but I'm trying to find equivalents), "Do these terms mean anything to you? Quietist? Activist? Handdara?"

"Very little, I think." Hanosz Prime smiled. "Nothing at all, actually."

"Well, then. You'd be wise not to let them remain mysterious for long, if you want to understand us."

"Father, perhaps this should wait until—" Kaivilda said tentatively.

"Please, child."

"And will you enlighten me, then?" Prime asked.

Kreidge drew a deep sigh. His gaze turned inward; he disappeared for a moment into a bottomless chasm of introspection. The subject was obviously painful to him; he seemed almost hesitant to pursue it, though he himself had introduced it. At length he said, "You've heard, I would think, of the recent supposition that the Earth, this entire galaxy, perhaps in time even the whole universe, is threatened by the expanding appetites of a devouring entity in a nearby region of space?"

Kaivilda's many eyes brimmed with sudden tears. A musical murmur of sound escaped her dorsal vents.

Obviously her father's barely suppressed anguish moved her deeply, Prime thought. A troubled rippling of the soft surface of her smooth ovoid body indicated that she would be glad to speak of something else, anything, if only she could.

Hanosz Prime, made uncomfortable by the unanticipated complexities of the conversation, shifted his position elaborately in a complex gesture that drew his bony crests and spiny protrusions into impressive interpenetrations.

"So it's looked upon here simply as a supposition, then?" he replied cautiously.

"Perhaps a stronger word should be used. The *theory*, let us say. But the theorists seem quite confident, at any rate, that some sort of great catastrophe does appear to be coming down upon us." Sinon Kreidge's face was pale and his boldly sculpted features were tightly drawn, now. The great bony ridges of his brows stood out like shelves of stone. "You people do know, out there in the—what is it called, the Parasol system?—what the recent findings indicate, don't you?"

"Yes, of course. Spectral lines are shifting toward the blue. The outermost stars are no longer fleeing the center of the galaxy. Apparently they now have begun moving a little closer instead. And perhaps other things are changing as well, out there on the borders of your galaxy, thousands of light-years from Earth."

"Things are changing, yes." There was a whipcrack tone of sarcasm in Kreidge's voice. He laughed: it was like a shower of sharp blades spilling to the stone floor. As Prime stared in dismay and disbelief, the older man seemed to go into a paroxysm of rising frenzy. Kreidge was flushed a bright crimson, now. Heat was coming from him in sizzling waves. His appearance grew more primitive—head drawing into shoulders, knees flexing, long arms dangling bestially; he could well have been retrogressing toward the dawn of the race even as he stood before them. "*Changing?* Disaster approaches, boy! Total disaster! The extremities of the galaxy are plunging toward us: that's what we're being told. Everything's shrinking together as the entity swallows up space! The sky is falling. The end is nigh. Destruction! Doom! Death!"

Sinon Kreidge sounded completely insane. His lips were drawn back in a frightful grimace. Driblets of spittle speckled his inward-sloping chin.

"Father—" Kaivilda murmured again.

But there was no halting him. "The movement of the spectral lines is quite evident, or so my sources tell me. The ancient light that reaches us from the most remote galaxies continues to be shifted toward the red, but the nearer stars of our own galaxy are plunging into the blue. The conclusion, my friend, seems inescapable. It's all folding inward. Things have begun to fall toward the center. Stellar distances are starting to diminish. The stars will come to embrace one another cheek by jowl; the sky will be a bowl of ineluctable light, and night will be as bright as day as the unstoppable End comes upon us." Kreidge's eyes had a furious manic gleam. His long gnarled arms flailed about in wild arcs. Spittle flecked his hairy cheeks. "Do you follow me? The End! The unstoppable End!"

He was making a spectacle of himself. Prime was appalled. Into a sudden pause in Kreidge's turbulent flow Prime said—something, anything, in almost frantic eagerness to ease the intensity of the moment, "You speak with great eloquence, sir."

As soon as he had said it he was afraid that his remark, which Kreidge would surely interpret as sarcasm, would create havoc. But Sinon Kreidge took no notice. He was too deep in the rhythms of his oration.

"At a certain point," he went on, "the process will become cataclysmic. The cosmic gases will be devoured by the inrushing forces of devastation. Molecules will be broken into atoms, and atoms into their component atomies. The pace of the destruction will accelerate from moment to moment, sweeping inexorably toward the terrible climax. Soon all will be a plasma: pure chaos. There will be an instant of unimaginable and immeasurable heat, and the sky will shiver and rend with a single frightful roaring sound, and then there will be nothing at all. Nothing! Nothing! Earth will disappear into that fearful maw. All our toil and striving wasted—all achievement rendered meaningless—every trace of the civilizations of a million million years destroyed as though they had never existed—not a speck left behind to mark our long presence here. Nothing will remain." His voice had become the tolling of a sepulchral bell. "Nothing. *Nothing!*"

"Nothing," said Hanosz Prime hollowly, simply for the sake of saying something.

"Nothing, sir. Nothing whatsoever. For us it will be utter devastation! The End of all, sir, do you see? The complete and final End."

And the ranting voice died away into ringing silence.

Moments passed. Sinon Kreidge stood stiff and twisted, like an agonized statue. His face was a distorted mask of torment. Hanosz Prime stared, astounded. He looked toward Kaivilda: she was pale, shivering with horror. No one spoke. Gradually Sinon Kreidge appeared to recompose himself, like a machine that had run amok and now was in the process of resetting its functions. The rugged planes of his face slowly adjusted themselves to a less dire expression. His posture grew more relaxed.

Then he said, in an altogether less apocalyptic tone, his normal voice restored, astonishingly casual, insinuatingly confiding: "Of course, there may be no reason to react with panic, you know. It may all be merely a false alarm. We here on Earth are very sharply divided, you must realize, over how to respond to these grim and horrifying speculations."

"Ah," said Hanosz Prime, baffled, and waited. "I see." Though actually he saw very little, except that the fear of death had driven Sinon Kreidge insane. The abrupt shift in Kreidge's manner seemed to him to be the hallmark of madness; though there was always the possibility that this was all some sort of game. In a noncommittal way Prime murmured, "The coming catastrophe. Opposing schools of thought. Activists—Quietists—"

What could any of this mean? he wondered.

"The folk who call themselves Quietists believe that there's little if anything that can be done, that we must simply wait placidly, go on living as we've always lived, and accept our doom, if doom is really coming, in a dignified way, without a whimper. Evolution's work is evidently complete, these people say: if that is so, then we should stand up and face the finish without demur. It's an honorable position, at the least, I have to admit. But some members of this faction go far beyond that. Rufiel Kisimir's particular variant on the Quietist theme is to argue that it's actually foolish to take any of these dire predictions seriously: nothing bad is likely to happen, because the universe is perfect and therefore imperishable, without beginning or end, by definition: it has always existed and always will. Therefore the signs of impending disaster that we think we see are most likely illusions or errors and there's no need for anyone to pay the slightest attention to them. Rufiel Kisimir—he practices some absurd sort of wizardry, you understand, that gives him, so he says, insight into the highest mysteries; no one takes this seriously but Rufiel Kisimir—draws these contemptible notions from the teachings of the Handdara, a band of idle philosophers who live in the snowy mountains of the far northern zone."

"I see," said Prime again, indistinctly. He felt utterly lost.

"Yes. Indeed, there's a certain unarguable beauty to their basic idea, wouldn't you say? I mean the notion of a perpetual and absolutely stable universe, flawless and forever incapable of knowing imperfection, that spans the entire arch of time. The arch is circular: can you picture it? It crosses from *here* to *there* and arrives at its own starting point: a universe that has neither a beginning nor an end."

"Beautiful, yes," observed Prime. His head was beginning to swim. "But is it true?"

Sinon Kreidge shrugged. "Who can say? The Handdara themselves haven't been able to demonstrate it mathematically. In fact, as I understand it, their most recent calculations seem to support quite the opposite conclusion. Which I pray that Rufiel Kisimir in his foolishness will some day come to see." Bit by bit Kreidge's manner was starting to seem crazed again. The darkness had begun to stream from him once more. It was deeper and more intense than ever. His face was fixed, rigid, edging into that manic look. Waves of insanity were spreading outward from his hooded eyes. Prime could feel the pressure of them. "Rufiel Kisimir thus far prefers to ignore the current news from the Handdara monastery," Sinon Kreidge went on. "He turns away from it; he closes his eyes to it. So he continues to yoke the most idealistic Handdara teachings to his own lazy-minded Quietist postures. Do nothing, he says. There's no need to worry. It can't happen and it isn't *going* to happen. Which seems to me to be offering a deplorably passive response to the grave cosmic situation that we find ourselves entering."

"So it seems to me also, father," offered Kaivilda with a curious urgency in her tone, and her smooth oval body quivered with feeling.

Prime felt far out of his depth. "Then I take it you both are Activists?"

Sinon Kreidge managed a frightening disconsolate smile.

"Not really. The Activist position seems based on a different set of extreme implausibilities. They say that there must be some way to fend off the doom—that we can find a way out, that we can deal with the problem somehow. The age-old primitive human response: fight on and on, against all odds, keep slashing away even though you're standing neck deep in a sea of your own blood. I find that equally hard to embrace. No, we reserve our judgment, my daughter and I."

"Often the wisest course to take," said Hanosz Prime uncomfortably.

"So we feel." Sinon Kreidge's voice was calm now, wondrously measured, but again there was an unmistakable look of terror and irredeemable desperation in his huge primordial eyes.

Prime, bothered by this new mercurial swing, felt a hot jolt of irritation. Where did the man actually stand on any of this? It was all too mysterious, too cloudy.

"What do you *really* believe, though?" Prime asked, in some exasperation.

"Ah," said Kreidge. "What do we really believe? A fine question!" He looked toward his daughter. "What do we really believe, Kaivilda? Tell him!"

Her lovely ovoid body swayed and rippled and elongated itself in evident stress.

"We believe—we believe—"

A pause, pregnant, taut. Kaivilda looked apprehensive. This was some sort of test, Prime realized. He had a sudden sense of Sinon Kreidge as a cruel and even monstrous old devil playing a demonic game.

"Perhaps—our guest—too soon, father, sharing all this with him—"

Her father gave her a ferocious scowl. Plainly that had been the wrong thing to say. Her voice trailed off helplessly. She caught her breath, struggled to recover her poise, looked off into the distance for a moment.

Then she said quickly, "We believe that the evidence is not yet all in. That surely there's much to learn yet about our predicament—if a predicament is actually what it is."

"Go on, Kaivilda," said Sinon Kreidge, with a menacing undertone in his voice. "You're doing very well."

Kaivilda continued. "We believe that it's too early to take a firm position. The Quietists may be right that the danger is total, that even to consider the possibility of a solution to the problem is foolish. Or the Handdara view may prevail: that in fact there isn't any problem. On the other hand, it may turn out that the Activist position is the proper one—that there's a means of salvation within easy grasp, and we only have to find it. And so we reserve our judgment, my father and I."

"Yes," said Sinon Kreidge. "Just so."

And beamed complacently at him as though Kaivilda had said something of great meaning and profundity.

It is, of course, no answer at all. Prime feels a growing queasiness. The increasing hysteria of this conversation is affecting him deeply. They seem to be hiding things from him. These are deeply troubled people, he realizes; there is torment here, and fear, and confusion. In just a few moments he has had all his expectations confirmed. The people of Earth are indeed terribly afraid of death; they are outraged by the prank that the cosmos intends to play on them, and it has driven them insane. This is more or less what he has come here to see; but now that he has seen it, he has all too quickly discovered that there is very little pleasure in the experience.

And he is beginning to experience something like the fear of imminent death himself, now, and that is a development he hadn't anticipated. Could Kreidge's gloom and Kaivilda's anxieties prove contagious?

Already Prime feels the galaxies pressing inward on him. Everything is tumbling inward. He is at the central point of the calamity and he will be crushed. It's a stifling sensation. He strains for breath. He needs to escape from these two at once.

He thanks Kaivilda for her explanation. And then he says, "If you would excuse me now—"

"Do we bore you?" Sinon Kreidge asks ominously.

"Hardly. But I'm afraid I am no philosopher, sir. These are matters to which I haven't given much deep consideration up till now. And perhaps my journey has tired me more than I realized at first."

"How unkind of us," said Kaivilda, "to subject you so soon after your arrival to such an outpouring of words, then. Shall we show you to your room?"

He is glad to be free of them. The first meeting has been an oppressive one. Not a good start, he thinks, not a good start at all. He had hoped for enlightenment here; but he sees now that the situation is even worse than he had expected, that these immortals have been transformed in a poisonous way by the intolerable awareness of their oncoming fate. And there is danger that they will infect him with their own unallayable anguish. He needs to be on guard against that.

SOME PARENTHETICAL OBSERVATIONS

(LOOK, GALACTIC CATASTROPHES HAPPEN all the time, and some of them are very catastrophic indeed, so don't get too complacent about the fact that the Ninth Mandala is a long time from now. Cosmic disaster is a fact of life, everywhere and in every era, and Kreidge and Prime and Heiss Vaneille and Rufiel Kisimir and the rest of the crowd aren't the only ones in danger, up there umpty zillion years from now. You may be facing some problems too. At this moment—here, now, in the twenty-first century which you and I currently inhabit—the deadly hypersingularity that threatens Ninth Mandala Earth is no bigger than an amoeba's pimple and absolutely no danger to us whatever, but nevertheless there's plenty of other trouble reasonably close at hand. For example, a tremendous war in heaven is going on right in our own cozy little Milky Way galaxy, practically next door to us. You don't know a thing about that, do you? But that doesn't mean it isn't happening.)

(It's happening, all right—in the constellations Eridanus and Hercules, and there's a pretty good skirmish taking place near the Crab Nebula, too. We know that because intense gamma radiation has been detected coming from quasars in those three parts of the sky. There have also been some gamma outbursts from a quasar in the constellation Virgo. Gamma rays are mighty mojo: they carry stronger energy than any other kind of electromagnetic radiation, a zap of 100 million electron volts per photon.)

(What's going on? Contending armies throwing thunderbolts at each other across the black reaches of galactic space? Well, maybe. A conflict between the Betelgeuse Empire and the Overlords of Rigel that has been going on for a thousand years and spans fifty thousand light-years—sure, that could be it. We aren't in a position to say, just yet. But simpler explanations are available. The likely thing is that these are purely random events: great chunks of matter and antimatter drifting together and annihilating each other in colossal bursts of energy, showering distant worlds with flashing streams of gamma rays. Just a routine example of the inherent violence of the cosmos.)

(Small stuff, really. Unless you happen to be living in the immediate vicinity of one of the explosions. Goes on all the time, hither and yon around the zodiac. We here on Earth have only just learned how to detect it, that's all.)

(Can it be that the universe is just warming up for the *big* catastrophe? Why not? Eventually all the little discrepancies that cause these noisy upheavals will be canceled out and the final act can begin. And then—then—well, why shouldn't the whole spectrum, ten or twenty billion years from now, start to slide toward the blue end? Why shouldn't the entire universe reverse the Big Bang that began it all and fall in on itself? There are no guarantees of comfort here, friend. People die. Trees die. Rabbits die.)

(Why not universes, too?)

(Look, there's nothing to be gained by going in for denial, my friend. Everything ends, even galaxies, even universes. Better to face up to it. Accept it like a man. Or a woman, or whatever you might happen to be. The sands are running out in the hourglass. You can dodge this way and that, you can come up with one subterfuge or another to keep your mind distracted, but the very likely fact is that even if you can manage to ward off personal bodily death and live on into the unutterably unimaginable far and distant future—and, like Hanosz Prime of Prime, you don't worry much about dying yet, not at your age, you know in your heart of hearts that it's never going to happen to *you*, don't you?—there's not going to be any way around the final collapse of the universe. I'm not talking about the little problem that Sinon Kreidge and his friends are facing. No, the Twisselman hypersingularity is just the beginning of the beginning of the end. There are worse things waiting. Entropy keeps on going up and up all the time. The quarks are quacking louder and louder. Day by day we are getting ourselves ready to drop back into the good old thermal equilibrium, where all things are one and everything is nice and calm; and none, I think, do there embrace. Your days are numbered, bozo, whether you like it or not. You and Sinon Kreidge have the same problem, and there's no hiding from it. Put away those megalomaniac fantasies of living forever that you secretly cherish. Hell, you may have no more than a few billion years left.)

HANOSZ PRIME THINKS THINGS OVER

LATER THAT DAY, ALONE in the fiber-cloaked resting-chamber that they have given him, Prime—thinking, contemplating, evaluating—spins in a gravity cradle of golden light, halfway between ceiling and floor. He drifts aloft, weightless, cradled on the air. The tension and distress that had begun to enfold him while he was with Kreidge and Kaivilda begin to leave him, now that he is free for the moment of Earth's iron pull.

He is not very surprised, of course, that Kreidge would be troubled by the predicted doom of his world. But he is amazed at the extent of his host's terror—and, now that he has been able to gain a little distance from Kreidge, Prime feels scornful of it, even. Where is the man's dignity? Where is his courage? Damn the man! Is death such an awful thing, after you've lived who knows how many hundreds of thousands of years?

That Kreidge would immediately plunge into a discussion of the impending destruction of the Earth and its galaxy, only moments after Prime's arrival, has made it abundantly clear to Prime just how much impact the news is having on these quasi-godlike beings. Back home in the Parasol system everyone probably knew by now that a blue shift appeared to be under way in the Old Galaxy and that that must mean trouble of some sort—but very likely hardly anyone wants to think about it and nobody is interested in talking about it. There's too much else to concern yourself with, and in any case it's just the Old Galaxy's problem, really. Even if what's happening in the Old Galaxy will eventually spread to other parts of the universe, it's going to take millions or billions of years to get there. Why worry?

But here among the immortals of Earth attitudes are evidently very different, as well they might be, Prime supposes. The lunatic relish and crazed gusto with which Sinon Kreidge had described the upcoming cataclysm—the stripping of the atoms, the frightful howl of the sky—is a measure of his morbid obsessive fascination with the whole thing. It is as if Kreidge can think of nothing else. He is in love with it, thinks Hanosz Prime. But also it has made him half insane. Kreidge is sick with the green sweaty fear of dying, of being compelled to give up a life that has already lasted—how long? Fifty encompassments, maybe? Hundreds of cycles? Half a mandala?—and which he had been smugly convinced would continue forever.

Poor Sinon Kreidge, Prime thinks, without much sincerity. Poor, poor, poor Sinon Kreidge. Sick with an old man's fears. Clinging to existence with all he has, an old man's savagely tenacious grip on life. To Prime it sounds like his grandfather all over again, but far worse. Was it really necessary to live forever? Wasn't it ever possible just to shrug and say, *All right, I've had quite enough now, here I am, haul me away?*

Prime is aware, more or less, that the contempt he feels for Kreidge arises from, above all else, the sublime cheeky indifference of youth toward age. Well, he *is* young—again—with all the cheerful know-it-all snottiness that goes with that. But maybe his irritation with the man stems from something a little deeper than that, he tells himself. After all, he has been older than he is now, and he has been a king, besides. He knows a little about dignity. It is the king in him that insists that Kreidge has no right to be taking such a woebegone view of the fate that is in store for him.

Then he wonders: What if they told you that *you* were going to die soon, like it or not? That there would be no more rebirths, no more anything for you? How would *you* feel?

He has no answer. The question is unreal. He's barely begun his life, really. A mere two rebirths? A couple of piddling centuries? What's that? There are people on this planet who have been alive for two or three whole mandalas, so the rumor goes. Maybe even Sinon Kreidge. Old enough to remember the great colonizing starflights of the Seventh. Prime can't even imagine what it would be like to live so much as an encompassment. He's simply too young. And so he can't imagine what it is to die, either—not really. A sleep? A forgetting? A blackness? Let me live another few lifetimes, Prime thinks. And then ask me again.

The hour of Earth's doom is still some thousands of years away, anyway. Perhaps even more than that: a million or two, even. In the cosmic scheme of things a million years is just an eyeblink, maybe, but to Hanosz Prime it seems like quite an ample span for getting everything done that a person might feel like doing. So why, Prime asks himself again, is Kreidge so troubled? He's lived more centuries than Prime has lived hours. Can he possibly have any unfulfilled desires left? Are there any worlds he hasn't seen, wines he hasn't drunk, thoughts he hasn't thought? Why can't he simply sit on his veranda and wink up at the stars as they come rushing down toward him? Don't you ever reach the point where you've had *enough*?

Evidently not. Poor Kreidge, Hanosz Prime thinks once more. Poor greedy Sinon Kreidge. To hell with him. All broken up about not being able to live forever.

But then Prime remembers—a murky shadowy feeling, but growing brighter moment by moment as the memory reassembles itself in his mind—how he had felt on the eve of his most recent rebirth: weary and grim, parched and shriveled of soul, hungry for new youth, eager to enter the tank and come forth reborn. It is an effort to do it, but he can, with just a little effort, cast his thoughts back to the time when he last was old. And then he realizes what's bothering Sinon Kreidge.

Only the old can truly understand the yearning for ever-lasting life, Prime tells himself. The young already think they have it.

He spins in his gravity cradle, midway between floor and ceiling, and a vast surging tide of compassion for Earth and its doomed people floods his spirit.

It catches him by surprise. He is amazed by his sudden change of attitude.

Of course they yearn to continue their lives. Their grand, privileged, eternal lives. Why not? Who would have it otherwise? And he remembers the strange words of Captain Tio Patcnact, the legend of which he had spoken, the king without a kingdom who comes to Earth to save its people from doom. Was it, he wonders, merely a legend? What if Earth could be saved after all? What if the collapse of the universe could be miraculously undone? What—it costs nothing to pile one fantasy on another—what if he himself, Hanosz Prime, former king of Prime, might be the miracle-worker, the veritable instrument of salvation? He thought he had come here on a whim, but no, what if it had been Destiny that had sent him?

Mere foolish sentimentality? No, Prime thinks. It must be his former self, his *older* self, breaking through the cheerful arrogance of his new youthfulness with a touch of the humanity of age—such age as he had attained before his last rebirth. Kreidge and his fellow Earthfolk have had a rare privilege, yes. But was that any reason why they should be punished, that the cup of life from which they had supped should be withdrawn from them, or, that if he had it in some way in his power to save them, he should not do it? Of *course* they yearned for more. Life is the most valuable thing there is. Who would willingly surrender it, even after a dozen man-dalas, if it still held the old savor? Why should anyone gladly give it up? Let Kreidge clutch it to his bosom as long as he could—as anyone would; as *he* would, if he were in Kreidge's position.

Poor Sinon Kreidge, Prime thinks one more time; but this time it is without any irony. And, spinning languidly in his gravity cradle, he gives himself up to a great access of joy, a feeling of gratitude that here in his newest time of rebirth he has been granted the opportunity to come to Old Earth and savor the intense pleasures offered by a world of immortals who have just discovered that they are going to die after all.

I will save them if I can, he tells himself.

His purposeless life instantly takes on new purpose. What delight! What ecstasy! He has never felt so alive before. He longs to explore the treasure-house of Sinon Kreidge. He longs to taste the joys of rapport with the beautiful Kaivilda. He longs to meet their friends, those gloomy aristocrats suddenly forced to contemplate the concept of doom in the sanctuary of their glorious castles. He resolves to wring the last drop of pleasure from this journey, and then to work the miracle that will spare them from destruction. Whatever may come, Hanosz Prime is open to it. And that, he realizes, is the particular delight and special wonder of being young…again.

Whatever may come.

Whatever.

Whatever.

Whatever.

Alvaro Zinos-Amaro and
When the Blue Shift Comes

Robert Silverberg

In 1987 I embarked on the ambitious project—too ambitious, as it turned out—of writing a novel, or series of novels, about the end of the universe. I would set it in an era of the far future so distant from ours that we could not even calculate how distant it was, and I would write it in a flamboyant, high-spirited postmodern style, using direct asides to the reader and other playful little postmodern touches, and I would carry the story on beyond the ultimate cataclysm into the birth of a successor universe. I called it WHEN THE BLUE SHIFT COMES and launched into it with an appropriate degree of vim and energy.

But very quickly all that vim and energy began to sputter out. By the time I was about 160 pages into the book I realized that it was fighting me, that the narrative line was wandering off in all directions, some of them quite unplanned by me, that in fact I had entirely lost control of the story and would need a thousand pages, or maybe a million, to bring it to any sort of satisfactory conclusion. I might not even be able to bring it to a satisfactory conclusion at all.

The experience was a painful one. It was something that had never happened to me before in a career that at that time had already come to span more than thirty years. In all those years, in all those innumerable writing projects, my rule had been that whatever I started, I would finish. Always. But not this time. Each new day's work brought nothing but more suffering and an increasingly incoherent story line. My wife and my agent and my friends and even my cats began to hear all about it as the daily ordeal went on and on. I struggled with the book another couple of weeks in ever-mounting anguish before admitting what everybody else, even the cats, already realized: I simply could not go on with it.

And so I abandoned it. I tucked the incomplete book away in a corner of my computer, out of sight and (mostly) out of mind. Now and then I would pull some pretty descriptive paragraph out of it and plug it into something else I was writing, but otherwise I left it hidden in a place where I wasn't likely to see it very often. And there it remained for a quarter of a century.

We jump forward now to January, 2012. My friend Mike Resnick tells me that he is editing a series of books under the general title of The Stellar Guild for a new publishing company, Shahid Mahmud's Arc Manor/Phoenix Pick. The Stellar Guild concept is that each book will contain two novella-length works, one by a well-known writer and a companion story by some protégé of that writer. Mike wants to know whether I am interested in taking part. And he dangles before me, as the writer of the companion story, a youngish European-American writer, Alvaro Zinos-Amaro.

I tell Mike something he already knows: I don't want to write a new novella for The Stellar Guild or anybody else. After close to sixty years as a professional writer, I simply want to kick back and take things easy, and, although I don't claim to have entered into a permanent retirement from writing fiction, I'm not interested in writing any books or stories just now and can't predict how long I'll go on feeling that way. On the other hand, the Zinos-Amaro angle is extremely interesting, because I know Alvaro Zinos-Amaro very well, consider him not exactly a protégé but a close friend, and feel great curiosity about what sort of companion novella he might be able to provide here.

Alvaro and I go back to 1998, when he was nineteen years old, a recent high-school graduate living in Munich and about to enter a Spanish university to study physics. (His father is American, his mother Spanish.) He had found my e-mail address somewhere and wanted to ask me a few questions about my writing. They were interesting questions, and I answered them in some detail. I was pleased not just with his interest in my work but with the intellectual depth of his questions, and told him, "To know that someone born in 1979 is on my wavelength is very rewarding. I wish there were more like you."

Before he left Munich Alvaro was kind enough to locate dozens of German anthologies containing my stories, books that I had looked for without success for many years. And back came more questions, too. Then the question-and-answer format gave way to a lively two-way e-mail conversation. Alvaro expressed a wish to visit California some day and meet me, and my wife, and my cats, and do some research in the ledgers I keep that record all the details of my professional career. The e-mails flew back and forth, discussing not only this or that bibliographical detail of my career but also what he, and I, were currently reading, and what I thought he should go on to read next, and our tastes in classical music, and all sorts of other topics, and before long, despite the gulf of more than four decades in our ages, we were on first-name terms with each other.

Eventually he graduated and moved to the States—to California, actually, though not the part of that huge state where I live. Inevitably, though, he made the 500-mile journey north to visit me. I was a little apprehensive about the visit—probably so was he—because it often happens that correspondents, when they finally meet, turn out to be incompatible in person. That was not the case with us. Everything about that visit went perfectly well, and we have seen each other many times since, both up here in the San Francisco area and in his territory in Southern California and at various science-fiction conventions in places like Denver and Reno.

And our e-mail correspondence, now in its fourteenth year, continues apace. Which is why I found the idea of Alvaro as my companion writer in a Stellar Guild book so appealing.

There were just two problems. I still didn't want to write a new novella, even for Alvaro's sake. And I had no idea what sort of fiction writer Alvaro might be. I had read some impressive critical essays of his, dealing with my work and the work of other writers, and there had been all that e-mail correspondence, and I had no doubts about his intelligence, his critical perspicacity, his knowledge of science fiction and his love of it. But none of that, by itself, qualifies anybody as a fiction writer. It helps, but what one really needs is the storytelling gift, the knack of seizing a reader's attention and holding tight to it, and all the intelligence in the world isn't sufficient if the knack simply isn't there.

I knew that Alvaro had had some stories published—in on-line science fiction magazines. But I am basically a twentieth-century guy in many respects, and I can't bring myself to read fiction on a computer screen. So, although Alvaro had sent me one or two of his published stories, I hadn't managed to read more than a few paragraphs of them. Perhaps he was a good writer, perhaps not, but I just didn't know.

As for my writing something new for this book series Mike Resnick was doing for Shahid Mahmud's company—

Well, no. No and no and no. I was adamant about that. But then I remembered the abortive BLUE SHIFT novel. I had been eighty or ninety pages into it, back there in 1987, before it began to go off the tracks. Could those introductory pages be salvaged and reshaped into a novella that would be coherent enough to allow Alvaro to write a continuation? I brought the unfinished torso of the novel out of its hiding place and looked through it. Yes, I thought: with a little polishing I could make those eighty or ninety pages into a stand-alone entity which, although it ended with the story left essentially in mid-air, would serve nicely as the opening section of a two-part novel. I described what I had to editor Resnick and publisher Mahmud. The idea seemed fine to them. Back came a contract.

Would Alvaro be able to work out a plausible conclusion for a book that had defeated as wily and experienced an old pro as Robert Silverberg?

I couldn't say. But it wasn't my problem, after all. I wasn't the editor of the series; I wasn't the publisher; I was just the author of the first part of that two-part book. Instead of solving the problems I had set forth, I had thrown up my hands in despair; but finishing the job was up to Alvaro, now. His intelligence and ambition and energy weren't open to question. Whether he was a storyteller too, we would all find out.

I made a point of not sending him my outline for the unwritten part of the original novel. It had led me into a blind alley and I was afraid it would do the same to him. He was on his own.

Months passed. I got occasional bulletins from him about the progress of the story, no details of the plot, merely indications that things were moving forward. And then the manuscript came. (He sent hard copy. He knew I would procrastinate forever if I had to look at the thing on my computer screen.)

With some trepidation, I began to read. And read and read and read. The trepidation vanished within a few paragraphs, and was quickly replaced by astonishment, by delight, by inward applause. On and on I went, amazed to see each dangling thread of unresolved plot that I had left behind me carefully taken in hand and dealt with logically—and done in a style that perfectly matched the prose of the earlier section. The story that had defeated me in 1987, that had trickled away from me into chaos, was now—now—

But I shouldn't attempt to influence the jury like this. Whether Alvaro Zinos-Amaro has satisfactorily tied up the bundle of loose ends that my novella bestowed on him is something that the readers will have to decide for themselves. I do offer, though, my own not entirely unbiased opinion that indeed he did.

WHEN THE
BLUE SHIFT COMES

Book Two
THE LAST
MANDALA SWEEPS

ALVARO ZINOS-AMARO

For my parents

♈

"I am dead, as you see, though I could have been immortal. [...] I consider pleasure to come from variety and change; but I was living on and on, and enjoying the same things—sun, light and food; the seasons were always the same, and everything came in its turn, one thing seeming to follow automatically upon another; and so I had too much of it all, for I found my pleasure not in always having the same thing, but also in doing quite without it."

—Lucian of Samosata,
Dialogues of the Dead

THE SONG OF LAST THINGS LAST:
AN ELEGIAC COUPLET AND
ONE MISCELLANEOUS STANZA

1.

WE ARE IN NEED of an ending. Heigh-ho!

Last things first; so began our song. And now off we go, to sing of last things last.

Before we reach those last things and that ending, we are in need of a continuation.

It can be arranged. It *will* be arranged—you're not so different from me (at least in *that* way): you appreciate continuity. Yes; one of the comforting illusions we cling to, even at a time like this.

I promise that you'll find out what happens to Hanosz Prime, and the immortals of Earth, and the Earth itself, and, for that matter, the entire blue-shifting universe—

All in due time, and in the due ending of due time.

But right now we must retreat. We must leave the Earth-to-come far behind and return to a world from which we departed, perhaps, too hastily.

For Hanosz, our hero, is not the only one to have learned a great deal about himself through his recent experiences. As you will see, seven hundred thousand parsecs away, in the Parasol system, Hanosz's brother Gililon (or Prime Two, as we shall call him), reluctant ruler, has also learned a great deal about himself. And like Hanosz, Prime Two has also made a vow regarding his future.

2.

IT HAS BEEN MANY WEEKS, maybe even months, since the snug little ship on which Hanosz darted away from his homeworld was within communications range of the capital's palace, a long time indeed since Hanosz sent his last message and parlayed his final wishes and suggestions to his sibling. A long time, therefore, since his brother Prime Two has experienced anything resembling joy or satisfaction.

We join him now as he drinks thick, syrupy wine from a stiff throne and observes the sun setting over the same thousand orange-tiled roofs, glittering white stucco walls, and towers of turquoise brick from whose sight his brother once drew comfort. But for Prime Two, the light that dances off those roofs and walls and shimmers, all-too-briefly, in the diffuse cerulean glow that accompanies the day's final throes, is far from reassuring. It is a reminder that another day has passed—another day of mistakes, ill-made decisions, loss of nerve. It is a reminder that he is one day farther along in a condition of existence into which he never thought he would venture for more than a passing moment in his adult life—the extraordinary, and extraordinarily dull and oppressive condition of *failure*.

Bitterly, Prime Two empties his cup with one unsavory gulp.

It amazes him that failure can take on a quality as sustained as that which he has come to know. Before Hanosz relinquished his responsibility and ordered him to become the absolute monarch of Prime, Prime Two had been sure that it was a terrible mistake. He pleaded, even when the pleading was so unbecoming that it made him question his own royal lineage. He begged, even when the begging made the pleading look like refined composure. He groveled, even as the groveling cast the begging in a courtly light. But all through this display of desperation, a tiny part of himself, a sliver of his mind, had held on to the secret notion that his concerns might be unjustified, that time would teach him the necessary techniques to rule, if not as wisely and well as his sibling, perhaps, then at least with a modicum of competence—in short, that things would work out somehow.

Over the last week that notion has been pulverized. Crisis upon crisis has wended its way from the common streets and cities up to the palatial grounds; crisis upon crisis has gone unresolved, indeed exacerbated by Prime Two's lack of wisdom and utter inability to lead his people. Prime Two is currently wearing a somewhat rare and unwieldy body-modularity known as Abidance—an unfashionable hybrid of something that looks like an ancient Earth black wildebeest crossed with a dromedary, adapted in this case for an upright gait. As he refills his cup, shame of the same unearthly color as the dwindling sun stings him just below his horns and works its way down to the tips of his long, hoofed limbs.

He sinks deeper into his throne and deeper into his despair.

He sucks down a long draft of the wine. It tastes tart in his mouth.

He closes his eyes and tries to imagine what Hanosz might be up to. But indignation and anger take over, stymieing the imaginative exercise.

Damn Hanosz! He may as well be dead, the self-centered ingrate!

With a twisted smile, Prime Two asks himself, for the thousandth time, why he has not been forcibly removed from power by those around him. The advisors, the administrators, those who siphon off wealth from the accumulated glories of an uninterrupted lineage that stretches back sixty-four golden generations to the Founder; the policy-enforcers, the commanders, the soldiers who are commanded; the servants, the fortune-tellers, the supplicants and the jokesters; those who praise him and those who critique him; and, most of all, the people, the people over whom he does not rule, but feigns to rule—Why, why in heaven's name, have they not rid themselves of him?

Are they too afraid to break with tradition? Are they too disbelieving of his incompetence to act against it? Are they so enamored of the notion of absolute monarchy and royal descent that they will allow their world to descend into chaos, as long as they have their royal king?

And for the thousandth time, the answer to Prime Two's question leads him to the same gloomy, inward-spiraling thought that has been crushing his spirit for the last miserable week. They deserve what they get. If they are willing prisoners to their own obeisance, let them suffer. If they are cowering idolaters, let them reap the consequences of their idolatry!

I am a fool, Prime Two muses. But more fools they.

He drinks.

He drinks some more.

There is no sleep, as we know it, in the year 777 of Cycle 888 of the 1111th Encompassment of the Ninth Mandala, but there is dreaming, and many other states of consciousness-aperture. Prime Two slips now into one such state, somewhere between exhausted reverie and confused dream, and he thinks *Nothing could be worse than this.*

At that precise moment, a communication alert thrusts him back to full consciousness. He is being contacted by Mirza-Mirza Ghasemi, Prime's High Ambassador to the Old Galaxy worlds.

Mirza-Mirza, ignoring Prime Two's bleary eyes and lethargic posture, says, with some agitation: "It's much worse than we thought!"

Prime Two grins a tired, wine-besotted grin. A joke, surely. Somehow, the Ambassador has tuned into his wandering mind and is attempting to lift his spirits through the ancient art of irony.

"How could it be any worse?" Prime Two asks, willing to play along for now.

"You remember the hole in space we detected?" Mirza-Mirza asks, straight-faced.

"Yes," Prime Two says. "Sort of."

He recalls it vaguely, worn down as he is by the chafing of his daily obligations. Hanosz mentioned it after he had left Prime, and Prime Two added it to the list of problems that he never expected to resolve during his reign, or for that matter his lifetime.

A hole in the cosmos? A rip in the continuum?

So what?

He has more pressing business to attend to.

"We have obtained new data that suggests the hole is growing at a rate far faster than originally estimated," the Ambassador says.

"How much faster? And why should I worry about it, when I can't even get the starship designers in Sibzamini province to end their labor strike? What will that do to our trade?"

Prime Two sits forward, then sinks back into his dejected slouch.

"At first we thought that the phenomenon posed only a direct threat to the Old Galaxy," the Ambassador says. "We believed it would take millennia or more to consume them. Since we're millions of light-years away, we assumed we were safe for much longer than that. But our logic may have been in error. The hole is so powerful, and is growing at such an accelerated rate, that it will devour the Old Galaxy—and everything within it, including the Earth—in centuries, perhaps even more quickly. Some think it will happen in decades, or maybe even in just a few years! The more mass the hole consumes, the faster it grows. If the most pessimistic forecasts come to bear, the anomaly could reach the Parasol system within our lifetimes—before your next rebirth, even. And that's not all. The intensity of the anomaly is such that it is sending ripples through all of space-time, additional tears in the continuum, ripping through a dozen galaxies. Our network of hyperwave channels is being destabilized. Soon we will have no faster-than-light communication with our outposts or neighbors. We'll be isolated."

"That seems oddly fitting," Prime Two observes quietly.

"Your Kingship, I recommend—"

"Recommend all you want," Prime Two cuts him off. "It doesn't matter. What could I possibly do? I've received your message. The news is grim. Quite so. We are in grave danger, and the danger is imminent, and we must face it alone—utterly alone. I understand. Is there anything else?"

"But sir—"

"You have made yourself clear. Is there anything else?"

The Ambassador, confused, shakes his head.

"Very well," Prime Two says, and discontinues the communication.

Night has fallen across the capital. The sky is littered with stars, more than can be counted with the naked eye, tauntingly luminescent. Furnaces of life, those distant stars; all of them to be extinguished, as it turns out, put out, ravaged by a hungry mouth in space—perhaps during his lifetime.

So be it. He will let the future attend to itself, and worry only about the present.

Prime Two begins drinking directly from the bottle.

3.

(THEY ARE ON TO SOMETHING, those who have observed the tremendous and unexpected growth of the singularity. They have stumbled on one of the most interesting features of a Twisselman hypersingularity: namely that, true to its imperialist form, it is shifty and deeply non-committal, quite capable of morphing into something far more insidious.)

(Twisselman himself, despite his glorious achievements in hypersingularity mechanics, did not live long enough to elucidate this aspect of the phenomenon. No; we have to wait for Mayerkind's work on phase-instability vacuum-subsumption for the principles behind *this* sort of transformation.

Mayerkind hasn't even been born, nor have his parents met, in your era; but they will, eventually, and he will, eventually, and after being alive for twenty-one years he'll realize one day that there are nine types of hypersingularity which, given the right conditions, can spontaneously mutate into nastier versions of themselves. The shift of the particular Twisselman hypersingularity that is threatening the Old Galaxy, and everything beyond it, was appropriately abrupt, as they tend to be; it occurred while Hanosz was having a nap, up there at Kalahide Keep, in the Ninth Mandala.)

(In its new form, the hypersingularity's growth no longer follows a linear function, or even an exponential function, or even a double-exponential—but a growth function of vertiginous and truly awe-inspiring speed known as an Ackerman function.)

(Observers in the Ninth Mandala have not yet had enough time to suspect this sort of expansion, and still believe that they are witnesses to a terror of merely exponential proportions.)

(They're wrong, and they're in for a nasty surprise.)

(Incidentally, this is what I meant when I said earlier that things would get worse. Everything is doomed to collapse into the Center of Things, yes; but this Center is an Ackerman-function vortex, not a simple hypersingularity, and nothing can stop that which possesses Ackerman speed—not even a hero like Hanosz).

WHITE DEATH

HANOSZ HAS TAKEN A LIKING to the gravity cradle in which he has had his insight about his purpose and the kind of person he is. We might be tempted to think that he developed this predilection *because* it was the place in which he achieved a sort of mental clarity, but we would be wrong. There's something physically tiring about Kalahide Keep, he's found; perhaps its position atop Mount Vorn, or perhaps the fact that it's part of Earth, and that *Earth* is tiring, after a time, to non-Earthfolk. Earth's gravity isn't to blame; Hanosz's body-modularity naturally adjusts for that, conveying to him the exact gravity-sense as that which he would have experienced back on Prime. Earth's wearying effect has to do with the same sunlight and air that help make it a perpetually self-renewing, self-invigorating ecosystem. For those who aren't Earthfolk, the sunlight dazzles, a tad too bright, and the air refreshes, a smidgeon too bracing. This, combined with the ardor that Hanosz feels for Kaivilda and Sinon Kreidge's tendency to lapse into histrionics at the drop of a hat, proves to be draining. Hanosz has no need for sleep but he does enjoy quietude and reflection—and privacy. Soon he develops what you might call a *habit*, thinking about the gravity cradle during odd moments when he isn't in it, and wishing he could luxuriate in it longer when he *is*.

This budding addiction is summarily shattered on his fourth night in Kalahide Keep.

The trouble begins when Hanosz hears a distinct grinding noise.

It's more than enough to pull him out of his introspection. The sound, close at hand, is accompanied by a tingling sensation that begins in his lower extremities and quickly spreads throughout his whole body-modularity.

Hanosz attempts to sit upright in the gravity cradle, a normally effortless procedure. But something pins him in place; the same something that first tingles, and now burns, inside him (a sensation that is inconceivable unless his body-modularity, which serves as a kind of armor, were broken); the same something that is causing the terrible grinding sound. If only he could determine its source…

He closes his eyes and listens, ignoring the burning that has become a blistering agony.

It's me, he realizes.

Devastatingly obvious, now; his own body is the source of the sound.

Those are *his* bones being crushed, *his* organs being compressed!

The gravity cradle is malfunctioning, then; the settings have been altered. It no longer buffers him from the inherent self-attractive force of matter; instead, it's now magnifying that force, creating an ever-steeper gravity well tugging him inwardly against himself.

He can't move.

Only precious seconds of consciousness remain before he turns into goo.

He tries to open his mouth, but it's impossible.

He attempts to unclasp his fingers, but can't even budge them a fraction of an inch.

A slipping sensation overcomes him then, a kind of liberating feeling, telling him to relinquish his hold on life.

Too soon, he thinks, and by now he's so mangled that the thought itself seems physically burdensome. *I have to save Earth! How ridiculous. I can't even save myself.*

And with that self-reproach—an unwitting parallel to his self-collapse—everything goes white.

He awakes in a nowhere place. He has no body.

But he isn't merely insubstantial; there's nothing around him; he's wrapped in something equally insubstantial, ensconced in a substance or state that lacks all dimensionality.

It's almost as nice as the gravity cradle, he thinks sardonically, trying to take a sunny approach to his new condition.

But that questionable optimism leaves him as quickly as it has arrived, and then he waits.

He waits a while longer, and then he gives up on waiting and simply exists.

Eventually, the whiteness returns—blinding this time—and he is no more.

The first thing he sees upon rematerialization is Kaivilda. Not a bad way to rejoin the living; not a bad way at all. At once he feels grounded in the familiar and the comforting, despite her inexpressive oval shape. The delicious prospect of rapport with Kaivilda that has been burgeoning since he has arrived at Kalahide Keep returns, unattenuated by his brush with non-existence.

"We're so glad you survived," she says, and her body produces the appropriate indications of this heartfelt relief.

"What happened to me?" Hanosz inquires.

He can talk again, apparently. He stretches his muscles. Even better, he can move, too. He's back inside his modularity—or a perfect replica of the one that has been gravitationally pulped.

"An attempt was made on your life," Sinon Kreidge says, jutting his frame forward. "One which you narrowly escaped."

"How...?"

"What's the last thing you remember?" Sinon asks gruffly.

"I was in the gravity cradle..."

"Good," Sinon says, as though the anticipation of a possible inconvenience had been lifted from him. "There have been no memory errors. Sometimes the reconstruction has a little glitch, you see. It's caused us to have to retrain several of the servants in the most menial—"

"Reconstruction? Servants?" Hanosz interrupts.

"What my father is trying to say," Kaivilda offers, "is that we're glad you were reconstituted from *equipoise* without any loss of memory-fidelity."

"What the hell was I doing in *equipoise*?"

Faster than he imagined possible, Hanosz's joy at existing is replaced with indignation. (Perhaps this is another one of Earth's side effects; to make one more temperamental.) What way is this for the immortal god-like Earth-dwellers to treat their guest, especially when their guest has been prophesied to represent their only shot at cosmic salvation?

"I demand a full account of what happened, and I demand to know why I've been abused in this fashion! Being shunted into *equipoise* against my will was barbarous; an act of outright hostility, one could say. I feel like I've been stripped of all dignity." He stops himself before his rhetoric has the chance to get away from him more than it already has, just now realizing that he is, for all intents and purposes, at the mercy of the quite-probably-insane Sinon, who stares at him impassively. So are his crew and ship, for that matter.

But then the improbable happens, and Sinon seems to soften.

"Quite right," Sinon says, and indicates approval with a vague clapping of the hands. "I would be just as outraged if I were in your position. Technically, though, it was the system we use to shunt individuals in and out of *equipoise* that saved you, so don't direct your rage at us. The system is programmed to constantly scan us and, in case of emergencies, remove us from danger at once. Still, you were treated unkindly, and you're right—it's our fault. The method of your attack leads me to believe that whoever was targeting you was unfamiliar with our *equipoise* redundancy protocols. And that means it couldn't have been Kaivilda or myself. If we'd wanted you removed, we could have arranged it in an infinity of more efficient—and far more diverting—ways."

It takes a moment, but Hanosz discerns why Sinon Kreidge is more animated, more friendly even than he's been of late. (And that last bit of bloodthirsty innuendo is just Sinon being Sinon; Hanosz has learned not to read any malice into such behavior.) Hanosz's improvised tantrum has sparked respect in the old patriarch. The aged creature is not only consumed by his own passions, it seems, but also thrives on the passions of those around him, perhaps borrowing strength from them.

"I promise," Sinon goes on, "to find out who is responsible and to take appropriate action. Your life was endangered; but more importantly, the sanctity of my castle was violated."

"Who could—"

"Rufiel Kisimir, that's who! The insolent, treacherous, deluded bungler! He must have received reports of your stay here. He must have been spying on us, overheard our conversations, become aware that you're quite serious in your belief that we can be saved, and that you will be the one to save us." Sinon doesn't bother to suppress smugness at this last statement; but then he dismisses his own dismissiveness, as though Hanosz's foolhardiness were no one's business but Hanosz's own. "Don't you see? You're a threat to his Quietist persuasions. You represent everything he dreads."

"But father," Kaivilda begins, and then stops.

"Don't interfere," Sinon says coolly. "You know how important it is for me to feel safe in my castle—to feel that *we* are both safe," he amends. "I'm going to pay Rufiel a visit."

And without waiting for a response from either Kaivilda or Hanosz, Simon Kreidge departs Kalahide Keep, leaving them to stare at one another across a silence pregnant with possibilities.

An Encomium to Tomorrow

"Don't mind my father," Kaivilda tells Hanosz. Her tone is demure. "This is his way of demonstrating his newfound appreciation for you."

"By leaving?"

"By acting out of a sense of nobility and seeking to avenge the wrongdoing you suffered. And"—more coquettish now, but still well within the realms of tasteful subtlety—"by allowing me to be your host and to ensure that your desires are satisfied."

Subtlety, you ask? Well, sure, to you this sounds pretty forthright, downright trampy maybe. But the problem is that the word "desires" in the Ninth Mandala has accrued such a rich tapestry of meanings that there is no clear correlative in your language, and it would take a long time to work through the network of semantic associations. What I *can* tell you with minimal effort is that when Kaivilda said this to Hanosz, the idea of rapport wasn't foremost on their minds (though, yes, there was an allusion to rapport—but a fraction of the one you might be inclined to assume). The principal meanings of "desires" in this context were that of journey-seeking, the adventurous consumption of metaphysical pleasures and the fulfillment that one derives from having a purpose.

And so Hanosz, after graciously accepting Kaivilda's offer to be his tour-guide, considers where they should begin.

There are countless splendors to see, a myriad of experiences waiting to inflame his senses, to engorge his appetite and become emblazoned in his memory so brightly that not even a century, or five centuries, or ten centuries, will dull their sheen.

But something weighs upon Hanosz; the psychological equivalent of a lingering subliminal recollection of the gravity cradle gone awry; a force that seems to direct him downward to the Earth.

The Earth, yes. The fount of life—of immortality—upon which he stands.

The place he should be…protecting.

Not touring.

The attempt on Hanosz's life is casting things in a new perspective, one harsher than he's accustomed to, but vitalizing in its way. He's alive. Isn't that sufficient cause for celebration? Does he really need to indulge himself when every moment of life is already a testament to the glories of the universe? He is to save this planet. Yes. Then why delay his fate? Isn't "desire" an elaborately cloaked shirking of his responsibility? The best way to embrace today is to realize the promise of tomorrow.

Knowing this, where ought he to go?

Kaivilda is waiting patiently for Hanosz's suggestion. She can see the symptoms of the inner dialogue Hanosz is conducting with himself: the intricate dance of suppositions, questions, and answers is manifested as a rippling in the quill-like protrusions and crests stemming from his multiple backs and wrists and knees and ankles and hips and loins, all of them pulsing at different speeds, undulating with their own shades of meaning.

Then the movement abates and Hanosz stands, statue-like.

"The Oracle Plain," he says. "That's where I'd like you to take me."

"Are you sure it's not too soon?" Kaivilda asks. "Remember, you risk—"

"—'troublesome disturbances of the soul,' as you put it," Hanosz recalls, playfully defusing her concern by acknowledging it. "I'm ready, Kaivilda. I don't expect that the prophetic wisdom of the Oracles will be more troublesome than my forced dematerialization, after all."

With the equivalent of a wink and a nod (an intricate double gyration of his Authentic hips), Hanosz reinforces his point, at the same time making it clear that he is not willing to reconsider his decision.

Kaivilda is mildly concerned, but amenable to his wishes, and respectful of his determination. (Simplicity and clarity of thought can often act as a precursor to rapport in the Ninth Mandala, and Hanosz certainly seems to be thinking simply and clearly—he has a mission, and he's eager to complete it. What could be more straightforward?)

And so they journey, nearly instantaneously, to the bleak and haunted landscape where the Oracles dwell.

No one on Earth in the Ninth Mandala has any accurate recollection of how long the Oracles have been around. A handful of Earth's denizens, those with an eccentric preoccupation with things past, would, if pressed, place the Oracles' origins back in the Fourth Mandala.

(One scholar with a penchant for purported accuracy that verges on the fetishistic would in fact insist that their appearance on Earth can be traced to the year 193 of Cycle 515 of the 944th Encompassment of the Fourth Mandala. But he hasn't been able to persuade anyone else that his dating system is accurate and, even though, against all odds, it turns out that he is correct, his reasoning is so convoluted that we will simply ignore it.)

The Fourth Mandala is a long time in the past for Hanosz; three full mandalas prior to the great starship exodus that colonized a billion worlds; two full mandalas prior to the creation of the incredibly ancient Vyeptos Station; a full mandala before the now-extinguished Serenities from which Kaivilda has borrowed her body-modularity.

Nevertheless, the Fourth Mandala is accepted by this informal cadre of amateur historians as the correct epoch, though the evidence that they rely on is tenuous, at best, and too recent to have gained any historical credibility of its own. It goes something like this:

A Star-Scrier of the 102nd Encompassment, one of those squat creatures with beady black eyes and a robust gift for mind-reading, created an amplifying device so powerful that it could penetrate into the minds not only of other living Scriers, but of the deceased as well. Quite accidentally the first Scrier to try this technology stumbled into the mind of a Scrier long-passed (how long, he was not sure), and in the mind of *that* Scrier found a remote link to the mind of a Seer, an altogether different sort of more ethereal creature with less predictable and quantifiable abilities. It was *this* Seer's memories that contained within them the dream of *another* Seer's experiences on a voyage of discovery to the homeworld of the Oracles. Needless to say, these recollections, based on dreams, filtered through a fragile Scrying connection to a dead Scrier, are not too trustworthy. But the Scrier became so fascinated with this alleged Oracle homeworld that when the connection with the deceased Scrier snapped, the shock was severe enough to trigger incurable dementia.

(Perhaps, then, you will think that the Earth history buffs are paying tribute to this tragic Scrier's sacrifice and immortalizing him with the choice of their date, acting out of emotional rather than strictly rational impulses. You might be right. Then again, nothing in the Ninth Mandala is strictly rational. Or strictly emotional, for that matter.)

The fragmentary surviving accounts of the Oracular homeworld—and no one had expected that the Oracles had their own separate planet, but why shouldn't they?—make it out to be a hellish, inhospitable place, like Venus with a nuclear fever, impossibly close to a neutron star and subject to radiation intense enough to strip the electrons off any self-respecting organic life-form.

The Oracles themselves are virtual creations of an odd sort; data-streams that once depended on hardware matrices to support their existence (systems that must have been designed by other beings, though no one knows who), but who are now capable of projecting themselves anywhere without an apparent source. An Oracle, then, is a creature of innate elegiac but also self-empowering characteristics; a fluid entity whose very immateriality is a testament to the sentience-generating feats of some lost and forgotten race, but also a reminder that any apparent limits to one's natural condition may be transcended.

Kaivilda has shared all this with Hanosz in the fraction of a quarter of an eye-blink required for them to reach the Plain. It helps Hanosz understand why the Plain is so barren, so deserted; the Earthfolk are honoring the environmental conditions of the Oracles' alleged homeworld, vaguely believing that it will make the Oracles more comfortable. Hanosz grasps something else, too; the Oracles are confined to this vast, searing plain; they cannot be projected outside of it; the Earthers have found a way to entrap them here. This oppression by one sentient race of another, real or not, is vaguely discomfiting for Hanosz. It's a tarnish on the golden hue of the Earth immortals. *But I should not be so quick to judge,* he thinks. *Perhaps they have their reasons.* Perhaps it is retribution for past transgressions committed by the Oracles. Or perhaps it is a preventive measure, for the Oracles have been known to demonstrate a tendency for endless, virus-like self-replication. (We will return to this theme.) Or perhaps it is for some other inscrutable purpose.

"Maybe you keep the Oracles confined here for my protection," Hanosz says.

"If only," Kaivilda says, neither amused nor displeased by his self-aggrandizing joke. "That would assume you'll find them useful."

"Wasn't it an Oracle who said that I would save the Earth? And don't the Oracles possess transtemporal divination?"

"An Oracle did say that we would be visited by a king who has no kingdom, and that this man would take the Earth on his shoulders and carry it to safety."

"Here I am," Hanosz quips.

Kaivilda is silent.

Since their arrival they've found the expanse uninhabited.

Where are the swirling hordes of virtuals she's described?

"They're shy around new visitors and render themselves invisible," Kaivilda says. "But they're here right now, passing right through us, as graceful as neutrinos. Give them a few moments to acclimatize themselves to your psyche."

Hanosz stares at the ground, populated here and there by twisted, gnarly plants only a few inches high, the earth riven with the marks of sand particles that ride violent night-time winds. Then he raises his gaze and studies the horizon. An endless procession of sand-dunes send up a parade of heat-pulsations through the shimmering air, baking the landscape, transforming it into a stifling, oppressive furnace. He imagines that he feels a little shove, one of those pulsations of sizzling air throttling him back a few steps, and then another, this time from behind, nudging him forward, and then another, more violent—

"They're testing you," Kaivilda says. "It's their way of being playful. Don't let them toy with you too much, or we'll get nothing out of them."

Hanosz tenses his body, burrowing his heels in, anchoring himself in place.

Out of a cloud of dust and sand a humanoid form coalesces, individual particles seeming to glitter with the reflections of a reddened sun, like tiny mirrors set afire, dancing in the air.

"You are the savior," the Oracle says, casting a deep, throbbing sound in the air that rumbles so that he can barely parse out the words. It doesn't speak; it envelops him with sound. "You are not the savior."

Hanosz turns to Kaivilda. She compresses the narrow tapered end of her egg shape and then releases it again, the equivalent of an unhelpful shrug.

"The Earth—" Hanosz begins.

"—will be carried to safety on your shoulders, yes," the Oracle finishes. It gyrates, a small whirlwind of activity that nearly knocks Hanosz to his knees.

"Hold on," Kaivilda warns. "Here they come!"

At the rate of about ten per second, additional floating humanoid shapes swarm around them, keeping a respectful distance of several feet at first, then hovering so close that their animated particles creep into the visitor's body-modularities, seeping into pores, climbing up nostrils, ingressing through all available means. Hanosz coughs, sputters, chokes, gasps, holds his limbs up to his ears and eyes, but the gold-like dust is everywhere, infiltrating every crevice of his modularity.

"Yes, yes, yes!" the Oracles roar, a multitude of unified voices, in the same deep terrifying pitch that seems to want to liquefy Hanosz's bones. The heat is getting to him now, the infernal blasted heat weakening his grasp on consciousness, on anything solid, anything real.

"You will save the Earth, and the Earth shall be destroyed!" they chant, ever more frenzied now, gathering into a maelstrom of flying golden dust, a vast, all-encompassing shape with no end and no beginning. The voice becomes many voices, and the many voices become one; deafening, thunderous, ripping through Hanosz's body.

"The Earth will be preserved! The Earth's demise is assured!"

He can hardly see an inch in front of him. He's being raised up from the ground now, sucked into the center of this Oracle storm.

"We shall all endure! We all shall perish!"

He feels Kaivilda's hand on his ankle, trying to pull him down, and the wall of sound becomes so overpowering that his modularity begins to shut down his conscious processes—he manages to get a glance of Kaivilda, struggling like him—she nods—he accesses the pre-arranged exit command—

And they are back in Kalahide Keep.

Hanosz can barely stand. He staggers back from the experience.

The intensity of the savage Oracles has left his modularity utterly drained of strength, his mind on the brink of temporary collapse.

He reaches forward for support, and Kaivilda embraces him with her short stub-like arms, and he wraps himself around her ovoid contours.

A Jaunt up North

"That was unusual, even for them," Kaivilda whispers.

Hanosz gently releases her from the embrace and takes a few steps back.

"They were certainly emphatic," he says. "If only they'd made sense."

Kaivilda completes a counter-clockwise three-hundred-and-sixty-degree rotation, denoting concern.

"I was afraid something like this would happen. I wish you would have listened to me. To try and brave the Oracles after being here for less than a week…was reckless."

"You heard them," Hanosz says defensively. "It was gibberish; contradictions. No use at all. Better to have gotten it out of the way."

"Maybe if we'd waited…"

"How could that have possibly helped?" Hanosz wants to know.

"Perhaps…" her voice trails off again.

"Yes?" he inquires, sharply.

"Perhaps their behavior was related to your disposition," she says.

"My disposition?"

"The Oracles have been known to reflect the emotional state of whoever asks them questions. It's possible that their contradictory responses were merely a reflection of your own conflicted state."

"I'm conflicted?"

"Aren't you, Hanosz?" she asks. She's less timid about her theory now, gaining courage by the moment. "I'm not blaming you. Who *wouldn't* be conflicted? Oh, Hanosz! You've seen and heard and felt a lot since your arrival. Someone attempted to end your existence. You're in a strange environment, surrounded by immortals. And we've been telling you contrary things. We've been insisting, whenever you ask us what we believe, that there are reasons to support both the Quietist and the Activist positions. We've been telling you that it's reasonable to accept our doom *and* to resist it; to do nothing *and* to do everything in our power to escape. It's our fault, really."

Hanosz ponders her words. Could it be? Are the Oracles so sensitive to one's mental state? If he'd known this was the case, he might have performed calming exercises, tweaked his brain chemistry with the help of his modularity, focused on unifying his outlook before encountering them.

But then he would have merely been suppressing the chaos, wouldn't he? Underneath, he would have still been entertaining mutually exclusive notions—

None of it matters, he thinks.

What is clear is that he should have taken Kaivilda's warning more seriously. Kaivilda was well-intentioned; she tried to help him.

And now she's standing right before him, gazing into his being with tender eyes.

They are all alone in the belly of a vast, labyrinthine onyx serpent, a living palace coiled around the metal-encrusted peak of lofty Mount Vorn, surrounded by all the mysteries and wonders of *the* ancestral world.

He feels a chill. The pheromonal attraction to Kaivilda is undeniable. Ever since he held her moments before, his pulse has quickened, and it is still quickening right now.

Whatever he does, he will do it with her at his side. There may be much confusion to his present life, but on this one precept he is clear.

She assents, almost imperceptibly, as though following his train of thought.

And with that, he takes six steps back, and initiates rapport.

(I've stated as much before, but let me repeat it here, since this is an opportune moment: rapport is not sex, and rapport is not love, but an altogether different mode of expression and feeling.)

(As with most rituals and protocols of communication between sentient beings, rapport contains multiple stages. It begins with what Hanosz and Kaivilda think of as Immutability. The closest twenty-first century parallel is foreplay, but since Immutability doesn't lead to sex or arousal, it can't really be foreplay, can it?)

(The idea of Immutability is a rather basic one. To ensure you've chosen the best possible partner for rapport, and to test the depth of the attraction you feel for him/her/it, you push through the superficial things—the specifics of your body-modularity and your identity-matrix—and see whether a *click* still happens with your underlying essence. Now, this doesn't mean that you dispose of your body or your identity. That would not only be foolish, but also impractical, since all that would remain would be a disembodied being without identity, and therefore nothing much to hold on to at all.)

(No, the way that Immutability works is that you change your body-modularity and your identity-matrix a dozen times, or two dozen, or two hundred, or however many times you wish, while your prospective rapport-partner does the same, and you determine whether you still feel that spark of interest in each other as you run through this gamut of physical and emotional shells. If you *do*, then it means that your underlying self—that part of your being that cannot be quantified with matter or psychometrics—is truly attuned to the other being's underlying self, and the next stage of rapport is pretty much guaranteed to be cosmically fulfilling. If you *don't*, then you may not have chosen a partner with whom you will find ultimate, long-term satisfaction, but don't be discouraged. The next phase of rapport could still be highly pleasurable.)

(So that's the reason Hanosz stepped back, instead of forward, to initiate rapport, via Immutability. When you begin donning a sequence of radically diverse bodies and identities it's helpful to have a little maneuvering room.)

Hanosz shifts the parameters of his body-modularity first, and Kaivilda initiates her own transformation an instant later.

The first change Hanosz undertakes is to reduce the virility and grandiosity of his modularity by tucking in the shoulder arches and smoothing out the numerous bony protrusions, so that they become residual nubs instead of actual outgrowths. Next, the large muscle groups begin to shrink, and the bones themselves become malleable, quasi-gelatinous. He molds his body from a towering, aggressive black-skinned mass into a smooth, slender, tubular construct, with pale green skin, dark brown glistening eyes with purple striations, and two limbs that end in elegantly tapered manipulating tentacles. He has no mouth in this modularity, and communicates instead through laser-like pulses emanating from an intricate network of vein-like luminescent tubules that begin on his mid-back and stretch all the way to his face. This is the model known as the Althar, and it is a remarkably adventurous choice for Hanosz, considering this body's comparative meekness and subtlety when contrasted with the Authentic he was wearing minutes before. The identity-matrix alterations he performs are much less substantial than the outward changes; slight adjustments to the intensity of his spiritual hankerings and his physical passions, an insouciance of artistic creativity previously lacking, and an overall tempering of his instincts.

By the time he has finished ringing these changes Kaivilda has just about completed her own. If Hanosz has demonstrated boldness in his transition, Kaivilda is about to put him to shame.

Gone is the oval shape and gone are the masses of cream-colored flesh and the always-open, fiercely penetrating violet eyes. In their place is an enormous six-meter-tall, bristle-covered reddish creature that leans on four limbs, her thin forelegs ending in bony paws, her hind legs concluding in ten-digit hands with inch-long claws. The skull-like head could belong to the hybrid of what you would call a dog and a gibbon, but the tongue is ragged, spiked and completely black. In addition, there appears to be another, much smaller creature attached to her torso; some kind of parasite, of which only an engorged feeding tube is visible, protruding from a felt-like patch in her body and connected to the outermost point of its bulbous circumference. This is the model known as the Thayn Quobba (parasite included). Kaivilda's identity tweaks include an increase in psychological resilience, a strengthening of the affirmation of her own cultural values, and a heightening of her aggressiveness and desire for competition.

They stand before each other thus, in these new guises of the flesh and spirit, and they wait.

It hardly takes a moment for the spark to return.

Hanosz is deeply relieved. Kaivilda is satisfied as well, quite so.

This is an excellent start to the Immutability ritual.

Now on with the changes.

As Hanosz proceeds with his second modularity change, he increases the speed of the transformation, too, a little nudge to Kaivilda to keep up with him. She accepts his bait willingly and is soon out-performing him in the speed department.

Hanosz goes from the Althar to the modularity known as Concordium, and then shifts from the Concordium to the

Dragon Rat. It's only with his fourth change that he leaves physicality behind altogether, electing now a more abstract manifestation in terms of sonic and molecular vibrations, a truly antediluvian and obsolete modularity called Verse Chorus Verse. Kaivilda has abandoned bone and sinew one jump sooner than Hanosz, rendering herself as a constantly rearranging cloud of three hundred and twenty distinct aromas and smells, each of which corresponds to a specific image and tactile experience when translated via an associated synesthetic alphabet. So now we have a soundless gas hovering in front of an odorless sound. But it works. They wait a second; and once more their waiting is rewarded. It's undeniable. They *feel* the connection.

This is just the beginning, a prelude to the stream of body-hopping that rapidly ensues. One of the dictates of the exercise is that the pace of change must increase and their sensitivities must be able to keep up with it. The changes follow so quickly now that they run through three bodies in a minute, then nine, then a dozen, flickering from one physical form to another to another to another to—

"Enough!" booms a familiar voice.

Hanosz stumbles back. Kaivilda is also stunned. Only her father would have access to this particular courtship chamber and there's no reason he—

"I return with grave news," the voice continues, less stentorian now, and recognizable as that of Sinon Kreidge. "Kaivilda, leave us at once! I have an urgent matter to discuss with our guest."

"But father—"
"Now!" Sinon commands. Hanosz shuffles toward the chamber's exit, wondering if he should signal his ship and pilot, resting in *equipoise*, to prepare for a speedy exit.

"Stay where you are, Hanosz," Sinon instructs.

Hanosz obeys.

"Father, you're not well," Kaivilda says.

"Leave now, daughter, lest I decide to take matters into my own hands."

Kaivilda interposes herself between Hanosz and Sinon.

"Father, don't make a scene."

"I'll have you removed by force," Sinon says in a steely voice. "You have five seconds."

Kaivilda lets out a howl of uncharacteristic passion, as though she's been mortally wounded: "No!"

She shoves Sinon back with enough momentum to send him reeling to the ground.

Hanosz blinks disbelievingly. Even Sinon seems taken aback by the ferocity of her display, and only sluggishly returns to an upright position.

Then, still possessed by this demonic intensity, Kaivilda blurts out, "Hanosz, don't you see what's happening? It's my father! He's the one who tried to murder you! His trip was a charade! But now he's returned to finish the job! That's why he wants me to take off. He doesn't want any witnesses to his ghastly crime! He only failed last time because I interfered! I was the one who ensured the palace scans were activated in the room that contains the gravity chamber. And I was too ashamed to tell you that my own father was the culprit! But I can't play this game anymore! Come, we must go!"

Sinon activates some kind of control to restrain his maddened daughter, but it's too late.

Kaivilda has already engaged an emergency shunter and whisked Hanosz and herself away from the scene of the confrontation.

Kaivilda stares at him, and nods apologetically. "I'm so sorry you were exposed to that. There have been tensions between us for...too long. It was only a matter of time before things came to a head."

"But why would Sinon want to kill me, Kaivilda? Especially when he concedes, however grudgingly, that I may be the savior of Earth."

"You're young," she says simply. "You're young, and you're arrogant, and my father can't stomach the fact that someone like you would be the one to save him. So he'd rather not give you the chance. He's hated you since the moment you arrived."

Hanosz, for the first time since his departure from Prime what seems a lifetime ago, is at a loss for words.

Is she telling the truth? he wonders. Could I have been so distracted by my attraction to her that I was oblivious to Sinon's spite? He recalls vividly his initial impression of Sinon being insane, of having been *driven* to instability by his confrontation with the end of his treasured immortality. But one thing is insanity, an inability to apprehend the real world and to relate to it, and another is premeditated murder; the relinquishment of all ethical values, the careful planning of a crime, the setting in motion of a series of events the sole purpose of which is to obliterate a sentient life-form. Can the leap be made so readily between the former and the latter? The jump seems to demand such a profound shattering of values, assumptions—*truths*—that Hanosz isn't sure that he can fathom it, that he *wants* to fathom it.

He studies Kaivilda. The unreal gleam seems to have left her features. Her current modularity, an obscure affair called the Vulpius, includes twelve limbs that can be used as either legs or arms, a prehensile tail, and two patches of scale-like iridescent surfaces on her sides which can project three-dimensional representations of whatever she desires. The surfaces are currently dulled, projecting nothing. That is the appropriate etiquette for an exchange during a delicate moment, but it doesn't comfort Hanosz any.

"We'll be safe here," she says. "The students are currently in another building far from this one, and Rufiel Kisimir hasn't taken an interest in this place in decades."

And where is *here*? Hanosz asks himself.

He feels a chill, and this time it has nothing to do with his feelings for Kaivilda; it's freezing in this hall, at least twenty degrees colder than the chamber which they've just occupied. Damper, too. His modularity will need a few moments to adjust. Hanosz strolls toward the hall's only apparent source of light, a shaft of radiance stemming from the nearest corridor that turns out to be cast by a mirror, and then finds the *real* source—

A transparent energy field spans a window six times as tall as him and forty times as wide, and the window, he discovers, overlooks a steep mountainous drop. The sides of the mountain and the plains below are all covered in a mantle of luminous, wind-whipped snow, and as he looks up at the air itself, he sees that the whiteness is falling even now, a hypnotic swirl of glittering white flecks through which the sun is only partially visible.

He turns to peer back inside. He notices flowing inscriptions carved into the walls, an unusual aroma wafting in the air from a nearby chamber.

"The Handdara monastery," he concludes.

The Rapture of Rapport

KAIVILDA JOINS HIM by the window.

"We can wait out my father's little episode here without being disturbed," she says, not explaining why Sinon won't send a horde of virtual servants to arrest them and bring them back to Kalahide Keep.

Presumably, Hanosz speculates, because he doesn't know where they are.

Kaivilda seems to be preternaturally calm, given recent events.

She says, "Would you like a tour of the monastery, to pass the time?"

Hanosz, a little thrown off by the mundane nature of her offer, says, "Very well."

But he hardly pays attention to Kaivilda as she shows him the sights. No. He finds the whole exercise dull—and concerning. How can Kaivilda pass so quickly from a stage of frenzied agitation to one of stoic placidity? How can she blather on and on about the inscriptions and the purpose of the monastery when so many larger issues, like their future, loom unresolved? It feels staged, Hanosz decides. Contrived. And since he's not focused on her commentary anyway, and finds himself increasingly subject to a distracting array of suspicious thoughts about her recent behavior, he decides to partition off his mental resources and allocate the majority of his conscious processes to communicating with the Captain of his vessel, Tio Patcnact.

(In terms that may be more familiar to you, he's splitting his consciousness and sleep-walking through Kaivilda's tour, the way you may have entertained yourself through certain high-school classes. He retains enough control to nod, ask the occasional question, and project an air of preoccupation that all but behooves his situation. Meanwhile, the real brain power is being used to retrieve the codes that activate Tio Patcnact and to establish a two-way link with him that exists only within the confines of Hanosz's mind.)

"You sound concerned, Hanosz," Patcnact says by way of greeting. Hanosz can't disagree.

"I am," he says. "There's some bizarre stuff going on here. I'll share the relevant memories in a moment. But first, I need your help."

"Ever ready to serve," Patcnact replies.

"Are you still connected to the ship?"

"The ship is in *equipoise* suspension, but I can access its matrix, yes."

"How hard would it be to reconstitute the vessel without Sinon or Kaivilda noticing it?"

"Not hard," Patcnact says smoothly.

"Do it."

Less than a minute elapses. "Your ship is ready, awaiting you in orbit."

"That's a comforting thought," Hanosz says. "But I'm not quite ready to leave yet. Still, I need you to transfer yourself to the ship, and to access the ship's readings."

"I'm there," Patcnact says. "What I am looking for? The ship's scanning equipment is sophisticated, as you're well aware."

Hanosz smiles ruefully inside his head, appreciating Patcnact's moment of pride.

"I want you to tell me anything you can about the following," and after these words, he streams his recollection of the attempt on his life in the gravity cradle, the ensuing theory proposed by Sinon and the counter-allegations cast by Kaivilda.

"It will take a few moments to reconstruct that data," Patcnact says. His voice sounds different now, his words more studied, more serious.

"What's wrong?" Hanosz asks.

"While retrieving the information related to your request, the ship has updated me with a series of disturbing cosmic reports."

"Disturbing how?"

"I'm verifying them now," Patcnact replies, and that's all Hanosz needs to know that it must be bad indeed.

"I'm afraid it's pretty much incontrovertible," Patcnact confirms a moment later. "The instability that is threatening the Milky Way Galaxy is expanding much faster than previously surmised."

"How much faster?"

"Fast enough for us to make our departure sooner rather than later," Patcnact says.

"What are you talking about?"

"The anomaly is growing with monstrous speed. Apparently, its growth follows a type of function that makes regular exponential multiplication look like a snail's pace. Current projections place the destruction of this Solar System inside of a year."

"A year??"

"That's correct. And based on what's been gleaned so far from the anomaly's behavior, even that may be optimistic. It could be a matter of months, or weeks. Hyperwave channels have become hopelessly scrambled, and it's going to be increasingly difficult to obtain reliable data from now on. It's nearly impossible to tell how much time we have. We should leave. Now."

Hanosz takes this all in as best he can, while his body mechanically follows Kaivilda from one wing of the monastery to another. Reality seems to have taken on a new hardness, a new lack of malleability. Despite technology that you would describe as magical, despite being in the midst of creatures who have roamed the Earth for who knows how many thousands of years and who would naturally do so *forever*, if given the chance, time is running out for Hanosz, and for the Earth, and for everyone. And he dares not ask the next obvious set of questions—if the apocalypse has become imminent here, how long until it reaches—or perhaps *pulls in* is more appropriate—the Parasol System, and his beloved Prime? And what about the prophecies?

"The ship's analysis is complete," Patcnact says.

It takes Hanosz an instant to shake off his gloomy introspection. "Well?"

"Kaivilda has been telling you it was Sinon that did it, has she?"

"Right."

"There's not enough evidence to identify who tampered with the gravity cradle, but there is enough residual data to prove that it *wasn't* Sinon."

"One suspect down, a few thousand to go."

"Also, Kaivilda knows it wasn't Sinon."

"But she said—"

"She lied to you, Hanosz," Patcnact interrupts, in that endearingly blunt way of his.

"You're positive?"

"I am."

"If what you're saying is true, I should get back to her right away, and find out why she's trying to deceive me. At this point, the best way to find out will be through rapport."

"You should take precautions. At least—"

"I already have. Should another unfortunate accident befall me, three redundancy systems will be able to reform me within minutes, with imperceptible data degradation."

"What do you want me to do, in the meantime?"

"Do what you do best," Hanosz says. "Prepare our exit. Plot a course to safety."

"Anywhere in particular?"

"As far away from the hole in space as possible," Hanosz says. "See you soon, old friend."

Hanosz severs the link and redirects the totality of his cognitive abilities back to Kaivilda and the monastery. He spools up everything she's just explained and integrates it into his conscious short-term memory. In seconds he's fully up to speed.

"Kaivilda, this has been fascinating," he says, "but I've been thinking that maybe there's a better way to make use of our time away from Sinon."

This sounds sleazy even to him, not at all the elegant and sophisticated flirtation he'd hoped for. But poor Hanosz has been through a lot. Don't judge him too harshly.

"You seemed distracted on our tour," Kaivilda observes, coyly avoiding his innuendo.

Or is she? Perhaps the meaning of her words is that he was distracted because of her? There's only one way to find out.

"I know things are far from predictable right now," Hanosz says, "what with the fate of the cosmos hanging in the balance and all. But I quite enjoyed our Immutability…and I'd hate to not find out more about the connection it's revealed between us."

They are back by the force-field window and the sensuousness of its panoramic view.

Kaivilda drops the force-field. A cold wind washes over their bodies. The sight is so spectacular that neither of them budge.

The sun is in full mid-morning glory. Peering outside, Hanosz sees that they are at the peak of a deep elliptical canyon with walls of black stone curving out on either side. Only the occasionally jagged black crag protrudes through the omniscient blanket of snow. The sun is incredibly bright against this white carpet, bouncing off in a million luminescent pinpricks that look like diamonds. Hanosz had assumed that a monastery would be designed to instill peace, to promote introspection. But this doesn't feel humbling; quite the opposite. Observing this naturally-occurring (if that's what it is) amphitheatre of stone emboldens Hanosz, and he allows himself to assume the role he must play, to believe it. He has entered a kind of dream, he tells himself, a reality outside the reality of Kalahide Keep, *above it*, somehow, higher up in the realm of attainable experience. Many things are possible here, things that might be frowned upon down below. The backdrop of the snow-felted bowl-shaped mountains clings to the morning air like a bright canvas, and he breathes in deeply of this rough gelid air. Every surface and contour is unnaturally bright, delineated with an artist's precision. The air tastes different up here, more majestic, more regal.

Yes, a dream.

And Kaivilda is dreaming with him. Everything will be revealed once they share the dream.

"Do you see it?" she asks, and it is clear that she is as invigorated as him.

"It's beautiful," he says.

And so begins the rapture of their rapport.

(It would be foolish to attempt to describe the experience that followed in terms of what it actually entailed. It would take too long, for one, and by the end of it you and I would both be so exhausted that we would have missed the point entirely.)

(But perhaps there *is* a way of conveying the fullness of rapport. Let us sneak up on the concept and relay its essence through its negation. Let us capture the glories of what Hanosz and Kaivilda shared on that snowy morning in the deserted Handdara monastery by cataloging the various things that such a rapport *was not* like. Whatever is left over, however improbable, will suggest what their rapport *did* resemble.)

(And so—

(Their rapport was not like a prune;

Their rapport was not like a plan;

Their rapport was not like death, not even a little death;

Their rapport was not like claustrophobia, or like being trampled;

Their rapport was indubitably not like anything counterfeit;

Their rapport was not like a war of independence, or like sovereignty;

Their rapport was not like responsibility, nor was it like freedom;

Their rapport was not like temptation;

Everything else—*that's* what it was like.)

(Words like *intensity* can't begin to do justice to the boundless remainder with which we have identified our hero and heroine's rapport.)

(It follows that in a temporary union of such magnitude there would be room for many, many things.)

(It follows that in the course of such an exchange Hanosz might learn things about Kaivilda and Kaivilda might learn things about Hanosz that neither had anticipated or expected. Such is the price of baring one's soul to another.)

(Well, as fortune or a lack thereof might have it, one of the billion things that Hanosz learns about Kaivilda is enough to shake the core of his being, and to confirm Tio Patcnact's information.)

(It shakes Hanosz so profoundly that the spell, so to speak, is broken. At least for now.)

He knows the *what*, but he has pulled out of rapport before discovering the *why*.

Dumbly, the word tumbles from his lips: "Why?"

Kaivilda cannot hide her shame. (Shame is part of the price of discovering another being's soul, even in the Ninth Mandala.)

"I wanted to prove myself to father," she says.

"You have quite a way of demonstrating your filial devotion," Hanosz mutters.

"It wasn't devotion," Kaivilda says. "He would have never asked me to do such a thing. That was part of the point, really. I wanted to demonstrate that I'm capable of independent initiative. I wanted to please Sinon by doing something without having been asked, or told, to do it. I am sorry, Hanosz. I should have told you. I should have revealed the truth sooner. Forgive me. I beg you."

Hanosz is as wounded as might be expected of one in his position. Not only is he not appreciated by the people whom he has been foretold he will save; he has been betrayed by the one whom he considered his closest ally and spiritual partner.

The following question sounds simultaneously melodramatic and absurdly comical to him, but he asks it anyway: "How can you expect me to trust you after you tried to kill me?"

He shudders, shaking off the intimacy of their already-smoldering rapport. He wishes to undo it, though that is impossible. The ardor and the majesty cling to him. It's repulsive.

"Answer me," he insists, though he knows full well no answer is forthcoming.

"How can I trust you, Kaivilda?" he asks.

She looks away, timorous, self-conscious, clearly uncomfortable inside her modularity, inside her identity, inside the damaged, warped creature that she has become after too much servitude to her megalomaniacal father. Her many limbs seem to writhe without purpose in the air. The scales on her sides project the image of swirling dust-clouds, dark and menacing.

And again he asks her: "How can I trust you?"

Silently, Hanosz, whose back in his current configuration grows into a sort of rippling cape-like appendage one tenth of an inch thick, directs his deeply hooded eyes to look away from Kaivilda, and levitates off the ground and floats in place, red-furred arms crossed over his shoulders. In this modularity, known as the Vramen, this set of gestures is the equivalent of shedding tears.

Then, after the long and ponderous silence that follows, he says, "Please, take me back to Kalahide Keep," and so Kaivilda does.

Hanosz exchanges few words with Sinon upon his return, for what is there to say? Your daughter, the same one who sequestered me under false pretenses, inadvertently revealed during our tryst that she was the one who tried to obliterate me—did you know she did it in order to assert herself in your eyes? Besides, does he expect Sinon will be truly disturbed by any of this?

No. Of course not. The madness runs in the family.

So Hanosz barely strings together a few sentences and excuses himself to his guest room. There is no logical reason to remain in the palace, but he does so anyway. He is tired, and he wishes to let his mind roam freely. He wishes to affirm himself, to recuperate the inner sense of who he is, distinct and separate from those around him, and he doesn't like the idea of attempting such a degustation of the soul from within the confines of his little ship.

Besides, there is still the matter of saving Earth, and just because they've tried to off him doesn't mean he should give up.

Neither Sinon nor Kaivilda voice any objections to his stated intent; they seem nonplussed that he is staying. Perhaps they would be equally nonplussed if he left.

Forget them, Hanosz thinks.

In his guest chambers, he erects a protective field and shares the deactivation sequence only with Tio Patcnact, whom he asks to be on standby, should anyone care to intrude.

Then Hanosz nestles himself in silence and shadow and allows time to pass.

Who are you? Hanosz asks himself.

He begins a long descent.

Hanosz does not find serenity.

He is besieged by the dreaded whirlwinds and the glaring fire-thistles, by the sun-voices, by the molten, devouring lava in the streets, scorching everything in its path. Ash. Ash. All crumbling; all in ruins. Except—these are not the familiar streets of Prime. No. The flames are much closer. Inside Kala-hide Keep. On Earth. Spreading out radially from his chamber, turning the entire planet into an endless desert, finally blossoming in petals of all-consuming conflagration. Fire, titanic fire, wondrous fire, wraps up the whole globe in an incendiary inferno of sanguine oblivion. Nothing remains—

Hanosz struggles to return to himself, to re-immerse himself in his now-sensoria. He summons all the residual energy stored in his modularity merely to prop himself up on his furry hind-limbs. He is shaky. He feels aged, ravaged, a weak and diluted version of whom he normally perceives himself to be.

The apocalyptic dreams have never been this intense, this crippling.

Hanosz thinks back to his recent travails, wondering if any might be connected with this onerous development.

He dismisses the obvious candidates: the gravity-cradle ordeal, the discovery of betrayal through rapport, the non-sense declarations of the Oracles.

But...what of the Oracles themselves? Didn't Kaivilda warn him of their effects? Just thinking back on how they swarmed around him, and how deep inside his being their voice rattled, reminds him of the flames engulfing the Earth. And that desert he saw behind closed eyelids, like the barren Plain on which they dwell...

I must go back, he realizes.

I must return to the Plain of Oracles, and this time I must go alone.

Yes. He is certain.

He deactivates the security measures holding his chamber in a bubble. He informs Sinon and Kaivilda of his plans. Sinon studies him with a blend of contempt and admiration and performs the analog of a shrug. Kaivilda, on the other hand, is immediately and visibly distraught.

"Hanosz of Prime," she says solemnly, "if you don't succeed, there will be no returning. This time the damage will be irreversible."

"I must go," he says.

Back in the bleakness of the desert, Hanosz waits for the Oracles to confer their wisdom.

He doesn't have to wait long. A wind rises; a piercing sibilance howls through the gathering dust eddies; the heat penetrates his modularity and sinks into his soul; he boils and he melts and he surrenders.

The Oracles assail him.

"He has returned!" they roar. "He has never left! He has returned to where he was, and he is going where he has been!"

Hanosz clears his mind of everything but Hanosz.

The Oracles are perplexed by this. They throw bizarre images at him, attempt to shake his inner quietude with grotesque sensory bombs. They soak him in a kerosene of weirdness, then light a bonfire inside his head.

But he persists. He is calm. He is himself. Nothing else exists.

The more he denies the presence of the Oracles, the more intrigued—and respectful—they become.

"Yes," they say, and it is no longer a menacing, booming sound, but a more ruminative voice, as though from afar. "Yes, and maybe. Perhaps, and no. The traveler returns; the traveler departs. The traveler that was once beside him is now beyond him. He has passed through the mirror and into the light, passed from the light and into the reflection. None know where the traveler goes; not even himself."

The voice becomes fainter, receding into a distance that is still eerily close to Hanosz. Finally the voice splits into its multiple component voices, and the voices slip into a gentle babble, as of a stream or a creek, and the babble transforms into a murmur, and then the murmur is no more.

One Traveler Ponders the Fate of Another

HANOSZ REFLECTS ON THE ORACLES' final words day and night. He goes about the business of his existence in a dull, automatic way, consumed by the Oracles' parting diminuendo.

Sinon tempts Hanosz with distractions, and Hanosz allows himself to be distracted.

Kaivilda, after a suitable period of decorously apologetic overtures, demonstrates a renewed interest in him, and Hanosz—tentatively—reciprocates.

Throughout it all he cannot stop repeating the Oracles' words to himself. They become a mantra. And then they pass from mantra to meaningless drivel, and they stay that way for a long time.

One afternoon, Hanosz is making idle conversation with Sinon about his past acquaintances. Sinon has grown curious about Hanosz's previous life as an absolute monarch on Prime. It seems to amuse the Earth man, and Hanosz doesn't mind indulging him, even if his words are greeted by a sardonic detachment that hovers between derision and aloofness. Let Sinon have his fun—Hanosz is still trying to decipher the Oracles' meaning. As Sinon interrogates him (there's no polite way of describing their interaction), Hanosz feels a tingle in the deepest recesses of his consciousness, a sort of itch he does not know how to scratch. Perhaps entertaining Sinon's questions is actively helping him in his quest, bringing the feeling of unresolved nagging to full fruition, so that he can take whatever action is needed to remedy it.

"So, you say you had visitors in your court often?"

"Yes," Hanosz confirms. "All the time."

The itch in Hanosz's mind grows stronger.

"But how were you able to accommodate them all?"

"A monarch must make time for his people."

"Ah, yes. Of course. Especially when you don't live forever. I see. How did you decide who you would see first on any particular day?"

"We have a system whereby venerated members of the higher-ranking provinces—"

Hanosz thinks, *We're getting somewhere now, I can feel it. I just don't know where.*

"So you discriminated."

Hanosz's restlessness is so intense now it's nearly a physical sensation.

"Thoughtful selections are of key strategic value when making monarchical decisions."

Sinon stares at him, and with a quizzical tone approaching indignation inquires further: "But what about off-worlders? Surely, your native population would come first."

Hanosz begins his reply with "Even off-worlders would have the chance to—" and then stops himself.

"Yes?"

"Off-worlders," Hanosz repeats stupidly.

"Indeed?"

"Travelers," Hanosz says.

And then the prickling burn inside his mind disappears and he feels nothing but relief.

"That's it!" he exclaims.

"That's what?" Sinon asks.

"It all makes sense now!" Hanosz says.

Kaivilda, who has been observing their chat from a respectful distance, is drawn closer by the jubilation. One rarely sees Hanosz excited these days, after all, for good or for ill.

"Don't you see?" Hanosz insists. Then he realizes they cannot possibly have followed his internal leap of logic.

"The Oracles said, 'The traveler returns; the traveler departs. The traveler that was once beside him is now beyond him. He has passed through the mirror and into the light, passed from the light and into the reflection. None know where the traveler goes; not even himself.' But it wasn't me they were talking about! They were talking about another traveler, one who visited me on Prime some time ago. Yes! In fact, in a very real sense, he's the reason that I'm here."

"What do you mean by that?" Kaivilda says.

"His name was—still *is*, let us hope—Zereshk Poloi. He arrived on Prime with enticing stories of a fabulous Earth. He was the one who first whetted my appetite for Earth with his silken tongue. And, moreover, it was Zereshk who showed up right before my rebirthing, the very same process that fundamentally *changed* me and inspired me to abdicate the monarchy on Prime and to set off on my ship. Zereshk Poloi. Yes. No doubt. Zereshk Poloi. He's the one who has been orchestrating events all along, so that I would wind up here today."

It's difficult to tell whether Sinon and Kaivilda are impressed or merely concerned for Hanosz's mental well-being.

Hanosz's enthusiasm is difficult to contain, though.

"Don't you see?" he goes on hurriedly. "It's clear now. My mission is to find Zereshk. He has the answers I seek."

"And how do you propose to do that, Hanosz?" Kaivilda asks in a mellifluous tone.

"'He has passed through the mirror and into the light,'" he quotes. With a mental command he calls up Captain Tio Patcnact and explains his notion. The Captain listens intently, offering no skepticism but also providing no encouragement.

"Can you help me find him?" Hanosz asks. "Look for any records of where he was last seen, or try to find stellar phenomena that might correspond to the Oracles' description."

A long pause ensues.

"There's an obvious candidate for his location," Tio Patc-nact says.

"Well, what is it, man?"

"The hypersingularity," he replies. "I've just confirmed my suspicion with the ship's last astronomical readings before the hyperwave channels went haywire. That's where Zereshk was headed when he was last observed by another ship. If you wish to find your traveler, you're going to have to head directly toward the beast that's devouring the universe."

(Hanosz's reaction to this is a complex and contradictory one. We don't have time to explore it fully here. Suffice it to say, his trust in the Oracles' proclamations, and his certainty that he has interpreted them correctly, competed rather stiffly with his desire to save his own skin and go nowhere near the maelstrom of space-time annihilation.)

(He struggled, but in the end the former forces out-weighed the latter, and, crazily, he resolved to fly toward the hypersingularity. Before leaping to action though, he decided he owed himself a farewell gift, something that would calm his soul and arm him with the courage necessary to face the imminent lunacy.)

(After considering various enticing alternatives, Hanosz decided to join Sinon and Kaivilda on a trip to their plea-sure-gallery, specifically to the chamber where they connect themselves directly to the rhythms of the cosmos. That may not sound appealing to you or me, but Hanosz is entitled to his quirks, especially under this type of duress.)

HANOSZ PRIME LEAVES EARTH

UP THERE IN THE YEAR 777 of Cycle 888 of the 1111th Encompassment of the Ninth Mandala—which, by all indi-cations, is looking like it's going to be the *last* year of the *final* Cycle of the *concluding* Encompassment of the *terminal* Mandala—the Earth immortals and their guest plug in to the swaying undulations and the ethereal ripples of the universe with the same ease as that with which you emit a sigh.

Hanosz doesn't feel much at first. But the lull is followed by a warm pressure that builds *within* his body and finally crosses the divide to the world outside his physical self, completely drowning and enveloping him in fluid musicality. He can feel himself inside it and it inside him. Reality has become a membrane, and he has just pierced it with the most delicate melody. He has become a bridge connecting both sides. But that's merely the start. For the reality-as-membrane concept is itself, he discovers after a few minutes of an impossibly beautiful tonality, just another membrane, and if he focuses on what he can hear—on what he can *feel*, for they are fast becoming interchangeable—he can slip through this membrane, too, to a deeper level of reality, and then again, on and on.

This is like no music he's ever heard before. It bears as much resemblance to music as a dinghy does to a whole planet; they are both vessels, but the latter contains an infinity of ecosystems within it, including the entirety of the former. There are more patterns within this *music* than it's possible to grasp, a super-abundance of replicating structures and symmetries embedded inside other grander, more dazzling shapes and arrays and textures of sound. That's his first impression. Many others follow:

The music is a bounty of colors, every shade and every feeling;

The music isn't bound by linear scales, becoming larger as it gets smaller, and smaller as it gets larger;

There is no cardinality to the music, no up or down or right or left; it is a circumference whose center is Hanosz and whose outer diameter is nowhere and everywhere;

The interconnectedness and dependency of everything is but one strand woven into the whole of the music's tapestry;

And much else, besides.

As these realizations and others seep into Hanosz, he feels some trepidation at the fact that the experience is not in the least reassuring. He is not calmed; he is not fortified.

He is dazzled, yes; impressed; but the vastness of his present connectivity is vertiginous; he feels queasy; he feels tiny, insignificant. He feels a little like he did when he tried to assimilate all of Earth's history in a single download. And then he feels *worse*. He could pull out, of course, but he's not ready to admit defeat quite yet. So he pushes on.

With growing desperation he spreads his thoughts outward, hoping that Sinon or Kaivilda will provide comfort, or at least guidance.

You'll adapt, Kaivilda replies nonchalantly. *It's a little tricky at first. Just tune in to a specific pattern of sound you find particularly noteworthy and drown out the rest.*

Too many patterns, Hanosz sends back. His growing distress is clear. *Need help.*

Follow my lead, Kaivilda says.

She narrows in her apprehension of the cosmic sounds to an isolated band, a single frequency and pitch. Hanosz detects it vicariously through her, and then locates it on his own. It's not particularly pleasing, but he's in no position to be choosy. So he hones in on it as well, excluding everything else.

Almost immediately he finds he can't keep up the effort. *Too difficult*, he transmits. *All other sounds pushing back in.*

No response from Kaivilda. He wonders if he's lost her in the chaos, and will have to disconnect to preserve his sanity.

But she says, *Something's wrong. The band is changing in a way it shouldn't.*

Just my luck, Hanosz quips back.

Kaivilda's assessment is right, he discovers. What they've zoomed in on is altering, sliding, shifting into a different type of sound, one far less palatable, more chaotic and dissonant.

Father? Kaivilda calls out.

I hear it, Sinon replies at once, and the three of them are unified now in their perception of this onerous phenomenon. Knowing that he doesn't have to grapple with this alone does comfort Hanosz, at least a little.

Should we end the session now? he asks several moments later. Truly, he can't see the point to enduring more of this torture. The dissonance has erupted into a full-scale cacophony; shrill quivering staccato bursts of noise trying to needle into his brain and scramble his consciousness.

It's just nonsense, Hanosz says. *Noise. I'm out.*

Wait, Sinon replies. *I think I've deciphered it.*

What is it? Kaivilda asks, unsettled but unwilling to contradict Sinon's direction. *It's hurting me as well.*

Hanosz wonders whether Sinon is even hearing the same thing as them. It's reckless to go on like this. To hell with him, he can—

It's the hole in space, Sinon says, and his thoughts reveal pride, but also terror. *The hole that's ripping everything apart.*

Hanosz is staggered by the revelation. Yes. He can feel it now. This is the ruthless, all-consuming beast tearing away at reality; *this* is what it feels like.

His stomach turns. He wanted to find nourishment for his spirit before the tribulations that lie ahead. Instead he has come face to face (inside his mind) with the hideous deformity that he sought to avoid. What use is there in prolonging the experience, now that he understands it?

Some use, perhaps. He senses that Sinon, disbelieving once, has accepted the reality of the cataclysmic force that is going to rip his beloved world to smithereens, and with it any chance for true immortality. Kaivilda has also resigned herself to the truth. They've merely caught up with Hanosz on this front, of course, who has known that this was real for some time. But it's progress nonetheless. At least he won't have to try to convince them anymore, and they'll have to accept that he's not quite so deluded.

And something else, too. A subtlety to the discord, if subtlety can ever be associated with such a harsh expression of bedlam; there is intriguing information contained within the fracas, something that could prove useful nestled deep inside the sensory turbulence. It takes all of Hanosz's resources to delve into the howling long enough to explore this nugget of significance while keeping his faculties intact. But it's worth it, he soon learns. After his fleeting reconnaissance he flits back up to the surface of the churning uproar and shares his finding with Sinon and Kaivilda, who have studied his movement with morbid curiosity.

As matter is being crushed into the hole, something else is happening as well, he shares.

Yes, Kaivilda agrees. *I didn't get as close as you did to that sound, but I heard it too, almost too faint to perceive.*

Hanosz gropes his way toward coherence: *It feels like everything…is going somewhere else. It's not just being destroyed here, in our universe…it's being delivered elsewhere.*

Principles of conservation at work, Sinon pitches. *We were foolish not to think of it before.*

Could it be? Entire worlds devoured, and then spit out on the other side of a universe-pinching funnel?

Maybe it is so. And though it doesn't make his task any easier, it does provide the succor that Hanosz needs to get underway.

Hanosz is back in space, soon to leave the Earth system far behind. There's just one little item left to take care of.

"Sinon," he says, as a perfect replica of the man materializes on the main deck of Hanosz's vessel. "Thank you for entertaining this last request."

"Entertaining is easy," Sinon says. "Conceding is a different story."

"Let me get straight to the point," Hanosz says. "Now that you and Kaivilda are full-fledged Activists, I'm aware that you have a thousand things you're going to try and do to help your fellow Earthers, even those reluctant to believe you. You appreciate the importance of my mission now, as perhaps you weren't able to before. So I'm going to ask for your help. Kaivilda and I…well, despite everything that's happened…we've grown close…"

"So I've gathered," Sinon retorts with some gruffness.

"I don't know what I'm going to be up against as we get near the hypersingularity," Hanosz continues. "And Kaivilda could be a stabilizing influence, should—"

"I can't," Sinon says. The recreated version of him flickers for an instant, as though his refusal is so steadfast that it momentarily overloads the projection system.

"Let me explain—"

"You want her to join you," Sinon says. "I understand fully. But I won't be separated from my daughter, not at a time like this. And I can't come with you. Like you said, there's much to do here on Earth now. So the answer is no."

Hanosz shakes his head and chuckles.

Sinon glares at him with supercilious eyes.

"You think this is amusing?" Sinon challenges.

"In part," Hanosz says. "You didn't let me finish, and you've misunderstood. I know full well that you would never want to be separated from your daughter—and, more significantly from my perspective, that she wouldn't want to be separated from you. Like you pointed out, your place is here. Nonetheless, I could still benefit from her company, and I believe she wouldn't object to mine."

"What are you suggesting?"

Hanosz says, "Allow me to introduce you to the finest medic I know, Farfalla Vlinder. He helped me keep my sanity as we were approaching Earth."

Farfalla, as most natives of the Borboleta system's fourth planet, is an unimposing individual, almost comically squat but solidly built. His entrance is equally unimposing, earning him no more than a sideways glance from Sinon.

"I understand that your daughter," Farfalla says, in his gravelly voice, "is quite stunning."

"I can attest to that, Farfalla," Hanosz says, and sighs in a way that you would think of as lovesick, but which in the context of this conversation denotes merely respectful appreciation.

"Beautiful she is," Sinon says, his patience fading, "and she's in no need of a medic. What use do I have for Farfalla here?"

"I believe Hanosz wanted me to tell you a little bit about myself," Farfalla says. He does just that, concluding his biographical sketch with the words, "—so, as you can see, there are definitely advantages to allowing duplication in this fashion. The stipend it earned the me back home on Bolis was enough to support me and my family for a year. And once I'm done here, this me's memories will be joined with the other's, which will add to his experience and knowledge."

"Clever Hanosz," Sinon says now, with a nod of approval. "So this is what you're suggesting. That I authorize you to duplicate Kaivilda for use aboard your ship. One Kaivilda isn't enough! Fine! I'll consider it, as long as she agrees too."

"She has already consented," Hanosz says quietly.

"I don't know whether to be impressed by your diligence or angry at your surreptitiousness. I see you've thought of everything."

"Actually, there's one more detail for which I'd like your approval."

"Go on."

"I'd like a safety protocol to be incorporated in the duplicate. It won't affect Kaivilda's identity matrix in any significant way. In fact, you won't be able to tell that a safety enhancement was installed unless you know about it."

"How will this modification help ensure the duplicate's safety?" Sinon asks. "And besides, why should we be so concerned about a duplicate's safety?" He looks at Farfalla. "No offense," he adds.

"None taken," Farfalla says.

"I should have been clearer. The safety feature is not for *her*. It's for the rest of us."

Sinon explodes with laughter. "You didn't enjoy the murder attempt so much, eh?"

"Once was enough for this lifetime," Hanosz says.

"Very well. You shall have your duplicate, and you can modify it to remove whatever deadly impulses may still lurk within Kaivilda. Still, you'll be depriving yourself of one of the more vibrant aspects of her personality."

"I believe we'll have plenty of other interesting things to keep us occupied," Hanosz says. Farfalla expresses whole-hearted agreement.

"Peace be with you," Sinon says. He flickers once more, and this time disappears.

THE DESTRUCTION OF EARTH

THE CLOSER THEY GET to the source of universal collapse, the more paralyzing Hanosz's dreams become. *Isn't reality dire enough?* he asks himself bitterly.

When he is not dreaming, he battles fear, anxiety and lack of self-confidence. He tells himself he will not dream. But denying his mind the option for release from the tyranny of conscious thought proves even more burdening, tiresome, debilitating. And so he gives in, and allows himself to dream, and the dreams tear him apart.

In this particular investigation into nightmare he begins in the usual way, with the whirlwinds and the fire-thistles and the sun-voices and the fire in the streets (it has become a litany by now), but suddenly there is a surcease to all these apocalyptic elements, and he's left standing on a deserted street corner in the middle of the night.

He feels his feet warming, and as he looks down to the pavement his legs begin to shake, the asphalt beneath his feet rupturing. He wants to jump to safety, to leap onto an unaffected adjacent section of the street, but he is *glued* in place, *stuck* to the crumbling surface.

A tide of heat erupts from beneath, and then he realizes it's not just heat, but lava, returned now more ferocious than in any previous dream, shooting up to burn and tear the flesh from his limbs with geyser-strength, and he yells and—

"Hanosz, come back," Kaivilda is saying.

He breathes in deeply and returns to the real world, uncomforted by the transition, and less than reassured by the expression on Kaivilda's face.

"Something's wrong," he says.

Kaivilda's lack of answer is all the answer he needs. "Please come to the bridge."

They walk there together, in silence.

Captain Tio Patcnact stands up from his station and says, "Hanosz, it's too late. We've just received a report that confirms it. The Earth has been destroyed. The hypersingularity is way ahead of schedule—and vastly expanded. It won't take us long to meet it."

Hanosz experiences a strange emptying of himself. His emotions seem to drain out of him and escape into some nether-place (the same place into which this universe is apparently leaking?). He feels numb, exhausted, incapable of even the simplest act, such as formulating a response to Patcnact's briefing.

After a time he asks "Are you absolutely sure?" and Patcnact shows him the data, and Hanosz sees at once that it's irrefutable.

Yes. Yes. The unthinkable has happened. The Earth— gone. *The Earth! No more!* Kaivilda, gone. Sinon, gone. The mountains and the castles and the Oracles and the snows, gone. All of Earth's Lords and Ladies, gone. Immortality, gone. And everything else around it—the entire Earth-containing Solar System and several adjoining zones, either about to go, or also already lost.

Irretrievably lost.

Hanosz snaps back into himself. "We're too damned late," he says. "None of this matters anymore."

"Hanosz, please don't speak that way," Kaivilda says. "Not *all* of Earth is gone. We still have its history. I'm here—I carry some of its knowledge. It may be too late for them—but for us..." Then Kaivilda, confronted with the implications of her own words, stops herself. "The original Kaivilda from which I sprang is gone. Nothing can be done about that—by you, or by anyone else. But at least *I* am here, and that's thanks to you, Hanosz. The original Kaivilda and Sinon consented to it, and I'm grateful that they did, but it was your idea. And now that we're all that's left…I can think of no better way to honor their memories than by doing my best to help you in what remains of our journey."

Hanosz is touched. If this is a performance, he's fooled. Memories of his rapport with Kaivilda spring unbidden into his thoughts, momentarily providing a reprieve from the desolation of the dismal news.

As though she can sense what Hanosz is thinking (and maybe she can, for the duplicated Kaivilda retains every aspect of the original plus some enhancements, including the closeness of thought established during their rapport), Kaivilda says, "If I demonstrate my loyalty, it may inspire you to trust me again, as you once did."

And in the midst of the destruction, in the long, seemingly bottomless shadow of the obliteration of Earth—the fount of all human life and civilization—there is a glimmer of light as Hanosz allows himself to feel heartened by Kaivilda's words, and resolves not to hold against this Kaivilda the sins of her predecessor.

THE GREAT SHIMMERING FILM OF LIGHT

"This is as close as we can get without being torn apart," Captain Patcnact neutrally informs the crew. "We've approximated our position to the last recorded sighting of Zereshk Poloi's ship, adjusting for the reconfiguration that has occurred due to the relative collapse of space-time. There's no sign of Poloi or his vessel."

Hanosz absorbs the update with an air of abstracted melancholy.

There is a general stillness aboard the ship, a silence waiting to be filled—by what? His next orders?

Well, that's part of the trouble, one of the reasons why Hanosz is more disconsolate than apprehensive; wariness requires an anticipation of the immediate future that he currently lacks. Throughout the trip he has confided in everyone onboard the vessel about his experience with the Oracles and his interpretation of that experience.

But his hunch doesn't seem to have led anywhere—except the brink of hell.

"You look morose," Kaivilda observes unhelpfully. "Don't be. We've made it *this* far, after all."

Though well-intended, her observation only serves to deepen Hanosz's moroseness.

"Yes, yes we have," he says. He points toward the hole in space, the massive lurching void that is shredding the universe into non-existence. "And now that we're here, I'm not sure what comes next. I have no Oracles to consult. What if my intuition was wrong? What if I've simply expedited our doom?"

"May I suggest," Patcnact says, impatient but respectful, "that we adjust our course and position for the next several hours—days, even—to continually keep us on the brink of the hypersingularity, so that we may scan it and gather as much data as possible? We may be able to learn interesting things that help others stave off destruction."

"A wise suggestion, as always," Hanosz says, appropriately chastised for his self-pitying vacillation. "I'm not sure what I'd do without you. Thank you, Captain."

"May I join the Captain in his data-gathering?" Kaivilda asks.

"Be my guest," Hanosz says.

He retires to his quarters. His current state will be unhelpful to the crew's efforts to understand the anomaly. He needs to master his emotions to avoid spreading his glumness. His example, for good or ill, still matters.

In the privacy of his room he ponders why he feels so dejected. Sure, it's natural to be disappointed by the turn of events. It's natural to feel doubt about whether his notion of Zereshk Poloi's role in all this was ever justified. But something else is bothering him.

Could it be self-recrimination? For what, exactly? How hard should he be on himself, after all, even if he *did* commit a stupendous error? At least he tried. He conceived a plan and acted on it, collating all available data and trying to elucidate its meaning. He didn't force anyone to join him on this expedition. Everyone who's here came willingly. If they—

"I think we have something," Captain Patcnact relays to him via the ship's mind-whisper net.

"What is it?" Hanosz asks.

"It might be best if you join us here," Patcnact replies enigmatically.

Hanosz is back on the bridge in moments.

Patcnact wastes no time. "I apologize for the interruption, Hanosz, but we figured that you would only get the full impact by using the bridge's virtualization systems. We've discovered something that we can't explain at the edges of the anomaly. Kaivilda, would you do me the honors?"

With several deft commands Kaivilda activates a three-dimensional representation that envelops the bridge. This is the first step in the virtualization process. Next comes the illusory magnification of the bridge's proportions. It expands into a perfectly smooth black surface of non-reflective info-matter that seems to stretch as far as the eye can see. Finally, the earlier representation swells and takes center-stage in this compartmentalized cosmos of data analysis.

Hanosz studies the image. It's the anomaly, yes. He can make out wispy trails of cosmic stuff streaming into it; interstellar dust, perhaps, and asteroids, and planets and moons, and actual stars, and everything else that is in the anomaly's way—which is, in the end, Everything.

But when he studies the image more closely he sees a faint shimmering film of light between the anomaly and the edges of the cosmos. He magnifies further and the film expands.

The film seems to coat the very edges of the observable universe, which are now within measurable range, as the boundaries of the universe are being pulled *into* the grotesque hole.

"What is it?" Hanosz asks, unafraid to reveal his ignorance.

"We believe it's a holographic film," Patcnact says. "Some investigators into cosmic evolution and various information theories have long suspected that such a thing might exist. But we're the first to have ever observed it directly."

How could anyone else have discovered it, without reaching the very edge of existence? Hanosz asks himself. *Our place in history is assured*, his inner monologue continues drolly. *For as many hours as history lasts.* Then he pauses. The sarcasm is just a defense mechanism, he surmises, because he's completely out of his element. At least he's had the good sense to keep it to himself; he doesn't wish to rob Patcnact of his excitement at the find.

"And what's it doing here?" Hanosz asks. "Can we use it, in some way?"

Kaivilda seems as entranced as the Captain. "We believe it may be some kind of artifact."

"Artifact? You mean, someone or something *placed* it here?" Despite everything Hanosz has experienced since abdicating his throne on Prime, the suggestion stupefies him. Who would have the power to envelop the whole observable universe in a holographic film?

"It certainly appears artificial," Patcnact confirms.

"On what are you basing that assessment?"

"The holographic film seems to contain a vast amount of information within it," Patcnact reports. "Though we're too far from it to try and decipher it, we see the patterns. Definitely not random."

"It couldn't have evolved that way?"

"It *could* have," Kaivilda says, skepticism peeking from behind each syllable. "The only way to know for sure would be to decode its content. If we could understand what it represents, we'd be a lot closer to ascertaining its origin."

"Surely, it's too large." Hanosz is still struggling to envelop his mind around the film that envelops the All.

"Even deciphering a piece of it would be enormously helpful," Patcnact points out. "There may be repetitions which would enable us to know what the remainder says based on a sample."

Hanosz says, without irony, "That's one of the reasons you and I get along so well, Patcnact. Your irredeemable optimism."

Hanosz can tell from the Captain's gaze and movements that his mind is already dedicating itself to the analysis of the film.

"Well, let me know what you find," Hanosz says. Floating here in this artificial endless void has suddenly become unsettling. He longs for the enclosed space of his quarters, the familiar confines of its geometry.

"In order to read even a piece of the film, we need to get closer."

"How much closer?"

Patcnact and Kaivilda hesitate before replying.

"Too close for comfort," Kaivilda finally manages. "There's a chance we'd be pulled in."

"How much of a chance?" Hanosz asks.

"Our current estimates suggest a thirty-five percent probability that we would be destroyed," Kaivilda says. "And that's a rather optimistic assumption. We've seen how unpredictable the anomaly can be."

Hanosz studies the film of light.

"Are there any indications that the anomaly may be sentient?"

Patcnact and Kaivilda look at one another.

"No," Patcnact says. "Why do you ask?"

"Perhaps the film is an illusion," Hanosz suggests. "A fabrication produced by the anomaly in order to entice us inward. We should consider all possibilities."

"That is indeed an intriguing possibility we hadn't entertained," Kaivilda says. "But like the Captain said, there's no evidence to support it. Also, we will be pushed inward sooner or later anyway. It's just a matter of time."

"Very well. What other options do we have?"

"We can try and get closer to study the film, or turn around and get as far as possible and wait for the inevitable to come greet us."

"I just got through complimenting you for your optimism, Patcnact. Please don't make me out to be a liar."

"I'll do my best, sir."

"He's telling the truth," Kaivilda says. "Those are our basic choices."

Hanosz, queasier by the moment, decides he has gleaned all the useful information he can glean at present.

"There is one other alternative," he says, terminating his participation in the simulation and returning to the ship's quotidian bridge. "We can continue to wait."

Hanosz's companion and the Captain do an admirable job of hiding their disappointment, though Hanosz still senses it. He knows they hunger for action. But something—and maybe it's nothing more profound than his own immediate need to rid himself of his vertigo—tells Hanosz that the time for action has not yet arrived. Not wanting to leave them mired in the uncertainty of his irresoluteness, Hanosz adds, "I'll make a decision within three days," and leaves them on the bridge, dissatisfied, but alive.

For three days he seems to drift in and out of a world made of dreams. Everything about this voyage and his life aboard the ship becomes unreal. Kaivilda reaches out to him, and while he doesn't withdraw outright, he does not reach back out. She senses his aloofness and respects his privacy. He doesn't wish to expose her to what he can only describe as a sense of...disconnection. In this state, he questions everything, including his own values and identity. He challenges notions he's long held dear, and at the same time adopts ideas that have in the past seemed repellent. He's standing on shifting grounds. Whenever he thinks he has anything figured out, it undergoes an inversion. The smallest acts take on the greatest significance, and the greatest thoughts take on the smallest meaning.

For three days and three nights Hanosz loses his sense of perspective, and for the first time in his life, the loss doesn't concern him.

At the end of the third day, somewhat haggard, he traipses to the bridge and prepares to share his determination. The crew seems distracted. Perhaps they don't wish to hear his decision after all. Perhaps they've grown accustomed to not having a clearly defined future, and would prefer to remain suspended in that state forever.

"After much consideration—" Hanosz begins.

"We have something," Patcnact interrupts. "We wanted to verify our readings before alerting you, but I've just been able to confirm it."

Kaivilda stands close to him, beaming with a mix of pride and affection toward Hanosz. "It's a message, Hanosz. Almost too faint to detect, but a message nonetheless."

Hanosz wonders if his crew has contrived something to alter his decision, if they would be capable of engineering false evidence to sway his judgment. No, he thinks. It wouldn't be like them. His paranoia is a lingering aftereffect of his recent loss of perspective.

"Well, what does it say?" Hanosz asks.

Kaivilda activates the playback.

And with the very first few words Hanosz shakes with excitement, and finds himself catapulted back into his old self, into his familiar senses, fully restored, returned to the individual on whom he had given up.

A Little Information Incest

"FORMER RULER AND MY ONCE gracious host," the message begins, "it's me, Zereshk Poloi."

Hanosz studies the reactions of the other ship-members currently on the bridge. Kaivilda seems to be bathed in a halo of renewed hope. Farfalla (did the others invoke him to check up on Hanosz? Does Hanosz appear so outwardly deteriorated?) is grinning unabashedly, a rare sight indeed for a creature whose lips naturally curve in a downward slope. Strettin Sibzamini, one of the Captain's adjutants, has abandoned any pretense of busywork and, fully perking up, has crossed his long blue arms in front of his barrel-like chest and has deployed his second set of cartilaginous ear-folds; the message has his undivided attention as well. Even rock-like Patcnact has broken into a display of joy and eager anticipation (we omit the details of this demonstration here, as you from the twenty-first century, no matter how unconventional and liberal you may deem your inclinations and views, would find the Captain's display atrociously vulgar).

In short, they are all captivated. As is Hanosz.

"If you're hearing this message," Zereshk goes on, a disembodied yet familiar voice, "there is yet hope for you—for everyone in your world. Perhaps there is even hope for me! Before I attempt to answer your questions, let me explain one thing. This message is pre-recorded, but it is also interactive. If you improvise beyond the abilities of the algorithms I've used to try and anticipate your questions, it will simply reset. If you choose not to interact, the message will plough through its entire contents in linear fashion."

"That doesn't sound like much *fun*," Hanosz says tentatively, curious to test how interactive the message really is.

"Don't worry about fun," Zereshk says almost instantly. "That will come, in due time. Now just worry about the preservation of the information of the universe, why don't you? Because it *is* salvageable, like I said. If you've made it this far, you may yet make it all the way. But you're going to have to do something you're really reluctant to do, and you're going to have to do it based on precious little more than faith.

"Your first question is probably who I am—my *real* identity, not what you thought you knew of me—and why I arranged events so that you and your intrepid companions would end up at the edge of the universe trying to decode a holographic film so you can try and prevent the End of all Creation. (It's too late to prevent the Time of the Falling of the Stars, as you've no doubt observed.) Well, let me share the bad news first. You're not going to stop the End of all Creation. That must indeed occur. At least, that's what *I* think. Which brings me back to *who* I am.

"Hanosz Prime, former ruler of Prime, you've always thought of me as a traveler, a sort of vagabond of the stars, a kind of self-defined gypsy, if you will. All that is true. You may just never have realized *how far* I've travelled…To be blunt, I'm not from your universe. I'm from a parallel world, one whose fate is closely bound with that of your own. I'm from the side of Creation *into* which all the matter collapsing on your end is being poured."

Hanosz remembers his shared experience with Sinon and the original Kaivilda as they listened to the ravaging sounds of the anomaly, and the sensation of matter being funneled into some other, unknowable place. *That* is Zereshk's home? Then how—

"You think you have it bad, with the collapse and the destruction. You do. But my side has it bad too, with the inflation and the creation. Lest we become too caught up in our own woes, though, let me try to guess your next question. How could I have possibly crossed over from one side to another?"

Hanosz performs the equivalent of a nod.

"The truth is, technology is more advanced on our side. When we detected the intrusion of the hypersingularity, we traced its origins back to your side and I volunteered for the mission. I knew going in, mind you, that it would be a one-way trip—I'll get to that later. Anyway, once I was in your universe, I maneuvered events as best I could to lead you to Earth, and from Earth to the brink of the cosmic fissure. As you may have guessed, this orchestration is part of a greater plan.

"Hanosz, as part of that plan, I need you and your crew to create a map of the holographic film you've discovered. I then need you to record that map in its full detail."

"But," Hanosz cannot help himself from interrupting, "in order to do so we'll have to sacrifice our lives. What good could it possibly do to record the film, if such a recording is to be lost soon thereafter? And what in heavens does the film contain?"

"Excellent questions," Zereshk replies. "The holographic film contains nothing less than the total information of your universe."

No one says anything.

"You heard me correctly," Zereshk continues. "Every bit of information that defines your universe is contained in that shimmering field of light. In fact, the film *is*, in a very real sense, your universe, simply represented in a manner different from the one you're accustomed to with your sense-perceptions. Trust me on this point. Naturally, as a result, the amount of information in the film is truly gargantuan—but the good news is that it's not infinite. Also, the universe now is much smaller than it was a few mandalas ago, or even a few Encompassments ago, for that matter, and the efficiency of the data compression in the film is itself nearly infinite, far transcending the ordinary limitations of your space-time. All of which means that you *will* be able to store the data in your ship. Don't try to decode it. The data-compression is beyond your means to reverse. You don't have much time, either. So please initiate your recording as soon as we're done here."

"Now, that's just the first thing you're required to do if you want to save the All. The second thing, trivial by comparison, is to head for the very center of the hole once you've recorded the film, and blow yourselves up."

Hanosz didn't like where this was headed a minute ago. He likes it distinctly less now.

"And what, precisely, is that supposed to achieve?" he asks.

"This is the part that you must accept on faith. Once you enter the singularity, the film's information will, for an infinitesimally small period of time, be added to the information content of the already-existing holographic film. You and your ship will be disassembled immediately after. Your physical selves will naturally cease to exist. But the surge of information in the film—caused by all the information it already contains being *re-added* back to itself; an act of information incest, if you will, on the grandest imaginable scale—will trigger a massive instability and usher in the final throes of implosion. The result will be the annihilation of the singularity—*and* the annihilation of both universes, your side and mine. But despair not! A third *new* Universe will emerge, and the holographic film of *that* universe will contain all the data that leads to the reassembly of everything that has been lost over on your side. And if that goes as planned, at that time a new parallel reality (a fourth universe) will also be re-established, restoring me and my world to their rightful place."

Hanosz's head feels like it has been plucked from his shoulders and tossed into the maws in space. The torrent of Zereshk's words is like a random concatenation of sounds and images, meaningless particles shooting right past him, rather than lucid instructions that will lead them all to salvation.

"But if all this is true," Hanosz says, visibly struggling even to entertain such a hypothesis, "and you already knew about it in advance, why haven't you fixed it yourself?"

"I'm afraid I tried, in my own humble way, and failed," Zereshk says, his regret evident. "I did enter the singularity and was scattered in a billion directions. My recording must have been imperfect. But don't be alarmed. When I entered I knew that even in the worst case scenario my message would get imprinted on the holographic film, from which it's currently being projected, and that you would likely arrive to finish what I started."

And this last revelation sparks in Hanosz another question that has been burning within him ever since Zereshk's voice first sounded on the bridge, and which must be resolved before he can continue.

THE MYSTERY OF CHOICE; AN ACCIDENTAL PURPOSE?

THOUGH THIS IS A MOMENT of high tension indeed in Hanosz's odyssey, we break for a few instants so that we can fully lay out his question—which will have surely crossed your mind, just as it did his.

The question is: Why *Hanosz*?

What makes *him* so special?

Couldn't any other being, or a fleet of vessels for that matter, have completed the same mission? Why are Hanosz and his crew uniquely suited to record the holographic data and thus help preserve the information that will eventually enable the reconstruction of the universe (we presume)?

This is a good question. This is a profound question.

I believe you've earned the right for a fair warning when it's necessary, and so I ask you to take heed; learning the answer to this question will change a great many things, and may even diminish some of the sympathy you feel for Hanosz (if you feel any at all).

Now you've been warned. If you care to continue, join me, and we'll return to the ship and crew that are poised on the brink of ultimate destruction.

First Cause, Prime Cause

We meet Hanosz on the bridge, deep in thought. He has asked Kaivilda to pause the message, and she has gracefully complied, despite her pressing desire to know how it continues. She and the Captain and several others believe that the request stems from Hanosz's wish to assimilate and internalize what he has learned, to evaluate the relative merits and non-merits of Zereshk's outlandish proposal. They believe that Hanosz has entered an assessing mode. But Hanosz's ruminations are far from such an evaluation; he is concerned, instead, with the specific way in which Zereshk has delivered his message.

By this we don't mean the mechanics of the message's delivery—the recorded voice, embedded somewhere deep in the holographic film, the interactive heuristics, that sort of thing. Though these details are important, they're not what Hanosz is pondering.

No, Hanosz's mind is on something more immediate. Ever since the playback began, Hanosz has noticed certain details about Zereshk's speech—his inflections, his turns of phrase, the way he strings ideas together, even the manner in which he has anticipated Hanosz's inquiries. And Hanosz can only produce one adjective to describe the aggregate sensation resulting from the analysis of all these details: *familiar.*

Hanosz feels drawn to Zereshk's personality in a way he can't explain, and it troubles him.

Why should the man exert such a great influence on him?

It seems almost like Hanosz is predetermined to trust him, to believe that he is telling the truth and that his intentions are noble, his motives transparent. And yet there is strong evidence to support the contrary, at least with regard to that last statement, for Zereshk has operated underhandedly and at great distance for far longer than at first seemed plausible.

The reason that Hanosz trusts the man, he decides, is that the man reminds him of someone close to him, someone with whom he shares an undisputed kinship—there is that *familiarity* again. His brother? His father? His grandfather?

No. Someone else. The notion begins to creep through Hanosz's thoughts interstitially, not blooming into awareness but sneaking through the canals of his mind.

Think back, Hanosz tells himself.

He recollects Zereshk's visit on Prime. He recalls Zereshk's prediction regarding Kaivilda: "I suspect that to enter into rapport with her would be the experience of a lifetime." Yes. Quite so! Indeed, it has transformed Hanosz in ways he has yet to fathom. And it compelled him to set off with a second Kaivilda when he wasn't permitted to steal away with the original, and this new Kaivilda is also a startling creature of light. How accurate Zereshk's description—almost as though he *knew.* But how? Surely, he had never entered into rapport with her. Kaivilda and Sinon hardly mentioned Zereshk's visit; it must have made little impression on them.

Could it have been fanciful speculation? No. Something lingers behind those words.

Perhaps it's best to treat this situation as he did his second visit to the Oracles: clear his mind of all clutter.

The last days aboard his vessel have prepared Hanosz for this exercise in a way otherwise impossible.

And so when he empties his mind, that dawning awareness, that creeping notion, that flowering tendril of insight, breaks through almost immediately, snapping into certainty and knowledge, filling him with a strange delirious ecstasy—and disbelief.

For he knows now, without a doubt, who Zereshk is.

Zereshk is Hanosz from the other side.

Zereshk is another version of him.

And there's more. Hanosz shudders at the realization, for it sends him reeling toward another insight, one so much more bizarre (and so much more unfounded) that he fears voicing it even to himself.

If—if—if Zereshk is an alternate *him*, and he has travelled over to this side to investigate a rupture between worlds…is it possible that the very act of crossing from one side to another is what upset the balance between both universes and caused the rupture?

Is Hanosz responsible for the death of all Creation?

Wait a moment. Not so fast. We must expound a little on this circularity. We must sharpen our deductive blades and skin the self-consuming snake for the sake of understanding.

Hanosz's experience on the bridge is a singular one. The crew is befuddled by his behavior, for since he has asked that the message be paused, he has entered a sort of trance. He has become completely immobile, lost to his private ruminations.

They thought he was assessing, at the start, but they grew worried as time passed. Could the message have affected Hanosz in some insidious (maybe even irreversible) manner?

They shouldn't worry, for Hanosz is safe. But the thoughts he is thinking are beyond the crew's ability to follow at present, and they test even Hanosz's limits.

He has discovered something of undeniable import; a possibility that is egotistically irresistible; his own role as ultimate agent of change and doom in a tilting of cosmic balances. But it's not enough to dream, to intuit, to believe. He must flesh out the idea, solidify it with the twin verisimilitudes of contextual plausibility and predictive power.

Very well.

To begin with the obvious: How can the singularity have been *caused* by the parallel Hanosz/Zereshk leaping from their side to ours, if the leap occurred *in response* to an investigation of the singularity that already existed?

We can examine this question with our primitive mindset and arrive at the answer more quickly than poor Hanosz, for our ability to entertain nonsensical and contradictory thoughts supersedes his (and this is perhaps the only instance where such a talent serves us in good stead, rather than sending us off into paroxysms of self-conscious despair and the like). The answer for us is, in fact, quite simple: the events define a closed causal loop with no beginning and no end.

Run through it. Parallel Hanosz observes an anomaly. In order to investigate it he crosses over into the universe from which it seems to be originating (*our* universe). But the act of crossing over is itself what causes the anomaly, which now certainly exists. And so the serpent, deliciously and without repentance, devours its tail...

And this is where Hanosz's quasi-mystical inspiration becomes retro-actively predictive.

How could his alternate self cross over? Superior technology, he claimed.

Why wouldn't their levels of technology be comparable to ours?

Answer: there's nothing to suggest that the universes are perfectly time-synchronous.

You've been patient with the speculation so far, so I'm going to come straight out and tell you. This educated guess is also correct. The two sides are not time-synchronous. Even though time moves at the same rate in each, they're locked into slightly temporally-displaced relative chronologies. Their technology is, in consequence, advanced enough to permit a jump between universes.

And what about the anomaly itself? Recall that the first recorded detections of mass leaking out of our cosmos were in *our* far past. And yet the anomaly was caused in *their* present. So, in addition to the time asynchronicity, the anomaly endemically distorts time, like a desert mirage. Look from this vantage point, and you see this timescape; look from that angle, and you see that one. (In reality, the anomaly does more than give the appearance of existing simultaneously in different times; it actually unspools time itself.)

Phew. That's a lot to take in.

But Hanosz is rapidly developing the belief that he's right about this (though he admits he has no proof). He is sharply aware of how this new-found conviction separates him from the crew—from his friends. He's been standing on the bridge in silence without moving for an extended period now, and they will worry seriously if he doesn't provide some indication of lucidity soon. But even as he feels this temptation to break off his speculative reverie his mind scours his memories for additional impressions of Zereshk. Hanosz regresses back to Zereshk's last visit on Prime, and more specifically to the start of one of their last conversations during that visit. Hanosz was sour, then, and felt that the whole interaction was vaguely distasteful. At the time he chalked it up to tiredness, to his need for a rebirth. But now he identifies something else. That other him, disguised by a different body-modularity, was a version of himself—a creature with different experiences and more powerful technology, to be sure, but with a similar basic cognitive set-up. Hanosz, in those few moments of heightened self-awareness, must have become aware of something in Zereshk too close to home. Perhaps it was Zereshk's confidence and his outward good cheer. Good, Hanosz thinks. I was on to something even then, though I could have had no way of knowing what it was. *My mind is worth trusting*, he thinks.

With that validation, he returns to the present moment once more, committed to tackling the impossible.

THE PRIZE OF PERIL

IT MAY SEEM TO YOU that Hanosz has spent an awful long time wrapped up in his own thoughts. You might even conclude that he has been dithering. And if Hanosz is our hero, doesn't all this introspection seem a bit improbable—where's his decisiveness, his innate talent for resolving situations quickly?

But, as I'm sure you're fast becoming weary of hearing, things are different up there in the rapidly collapsing Ninth Mandala. Introspection *is* considered a form of action. And in that regard Hanosz has been very active indeed. Consider, too, how much is in the balance. If he makes the wrong choice, he may never be able to redeem himself.

Redeem himself, you ask? Yes. Atone for his sins. For isn't it Hanosz, or a version thereof, who has unleashed the apocalypse? Isn't our Hanosz merely trying to right the equilibrium that his reflection upset?

The person from whom Hanosz feels the most pressure to make the right decision is himself. But in a way, he realizes, this is nonsense, for the universe (himself included) won't be around to express disappointment if he gets it wrong.

He shouldn't, therefore, strive to restore what has been ruined, to seal what has been breached.

He should strive to free himself from his own expectations and do what must be done.

Hanosz says, "Let us proceed with the rest of the message."

Relieved, Kaivilda does as instructed.

When it's over, Hanosz says, "The meaning of this message is plain, as is plain what must happen next."

"Forgive me, Hanosz," Kaivilda says, "but how can we be sure it's true?"

Hanosz, unshackled now from caring about what he thinks of his own performance, is careful not to do anything with his body language that might project this and have it be mistaken as recklessness or a desire to self-destruct.

"A legitimate question," he says, "for which I don't have a satisfying, empirically verifiable answer. My intuition tells me it's the right thing to do, and I've come to trust my intuition."

"That's it?" Farfalla asks.

"We must take the risk so that we have a chance of preserving everything we value," Hanosz says. "To end the suffering of two universes that have been fatally punctured. If we attempt to retreat, we know for a fact that we will be destroyed—though we may not know the exact moment, it will happen, and soon. So let us accept our own imminent annihilation. It is unquestionable. There is no hope for salvation. But if that's true, what possible loss could there be in embracing it? Why not extinguish ourselves now willingly rather than waiting for the cruelty to be imposed upon us by a Creation torn asunder?"

A curious thing happens to Hanosz then. For all of the certainty and eloquence with which he's preaching, he feels his own faith in his message crumbling right before him. What if he *is* wrong? What if they can head back and find a mysterious safe zone, some unaffected area in which to live out the rest of their days? The scientists could be wrong, couldn't they? If a universe can contain a hole in its center that sucks its very essence away, might it also not contain a protrusion, a galaxy-shaped nodule that will forever remain outside the collapse?

"Hanosz," Kaivilda says, "I have another update for you." She seems reluctant to continue.

Hanosz prods her with his eyes.

"Prime is gone," she says.

First Earth.

Now Prime.

His brother. His people.

The entire Parasol system. The moons he saw from Prime on a clear summer night sky so long ago, as his father taught him the ways of monarchy.

No more.

—In this universe, even if a safe zone does exist, it's not worth living in.

"We will do as Zereshk has asked in his message," Hanosz declares in a flat voice. Hanosz sees no need to explain *everything* to his crew. The message has covered all the essentials, except for the part about Zereshk being a parallel version of Hanosz. "If you don't wish to proceed, you may abandon ship now in one of the emergency vessels, and my best wishes to you. Whoever stays here with me is going to finish recording the hologram. And then we're going inside the beast. My mind's made up."

DAY ZERO

IT'S NO LONGER THE NINTH MANDALA; all such conventional measures of time have ceased to hold meaning, as Hanosz's universe and that of his counterpart have been obliterated. (Hanosz himself, of course, and everyone else we've met so far, has also been rubbed out.)

Instead, we have a new universe, just emerged from the ashes of the previous two. This new universe engages in the sort of tantrum common to most newborn universes, inflating by fits and starts, flirting with extra dimensions, violating all kinds of principles, experimenting with dark this and dark that, shaking out the quirks of its fundamental physics (and thereby assuring that the smartest minds which under normal circumstances would eventually evolve, millions of years hence, would spend a good deal of time trying to figure out what the heck happened in those initial few instants—if the normal course of cosmic evolution were to occur, which it is not).

Another thing that this new cosmos does (also not uncommon for toddler universes) is to duplicate its entire information content in the form of a holographic film. Don't ask why—universes just do this sort of thing.

The film presently begins the humdrum process of settling over the cosmological horizon, not unlike skin settling over boiled milk.

The infancy pangs of any universe (should you or any other sentient creature somehow be able to exist *outside* of it and observe them) would be enough to melt your heart, or at least make you quiver.

But *this* new universe in particular deserves your awe and empathy, for it experiences an unprecedented hiccup (which, since it affects its entirety, can be said without exaggeration to have cosmic proportions) in the settling phase of the holographic film.

An irregularity arises; a bump; a swell.

This is the bubble of information that Hanosz and his crew, through their act of disintegration by hypersingularity, have programmed into the former film.

This quirk, this bubble, expands, and grows precipitously until it encompasses the entire film, and then takes it over. I'll have more to say about this in a moment.

But first, a problem.

If Hanosz and Kaivilda and the others could witness this, they might cheer. Hanosz Prime was right! they might think, and they might be overcome with exuberant relief, indescribable joy.

If so, they would be celebrating prematurely.

For there's a hitch; a little side effect of the film reconfiguration that none of them could have predicted.

The universe at the time of the bubble takeover is still young. It is, therefore, still hot, very hot, and chock full of radiation, a veritable super-heated soup of elemental forces and particles. As the information bubble expands to encompass the entire cosmological horizon, it interacts, in an unforeseen way, with this radiation, casting it here and there, flinging it where it would otherwise not have been flung.

Mind you, this entire process, including the radiation-grazing and dispersion phenomenon, occurs in less than a billionth of a billionth of a billionth of a femto-second (never mind Encompassments!)—but it does have long-term consequences.

One such consequence is that the entire contents of the newly hatched universe are exposed to levels of radiation higher than the ones in Hanosz's former habitat.

Fret not, though. Higher does not mean terminal, nor does it mean life-precluding; it simply means higher. On the whole, average radiation levels end up being only one billionth of a billionth of a billionth of a pico-roentgen more than they were in Hanosz's former universe.

But sometimes that's all it takes.

And now back to the bubble's effect on the film. It takes it over, yes. Completely.

That is to say, the original holographic film is wholeheartedly altered.

Altered how? you ask. Why, in precisely the manner that Hanosz had hoped for:

The film now replicates the exact configuration of Hanosz's previous universe as it was prior to the emergence of the hypersingularity. As a result, this new universe does not require millions of years to generate stars, planets, and sentience; it does so at once. It has no choice. Think of the physical universe in this instance as what you would call a software simulation; change the underlying code (or, in this case, the holographic data), and the simulation will be altered instantly to reflect the changes.

And so the universe pops into being, fully restored, like a ready-made flan, coalescing into a state it would have taken eons to arrive at naturally, with Hanosz and the others merrily going about their business, and quite oblivious as to what has happened.

And what's best of all, nary a sign of the hypersingularity.

The Oracles, it turns out, were right. (They have an annoying tendency to be right, even when I throw them for a loop. More on that later.)

The Oracles said:

"You will save the Earth, and the Earth shall be destroyed!"

They said:

"The Earth will be preserved! The Earth's demise is assured!"

And so it has come to pass.

The lesson should be clear. If there are any true mechanisms of transtemporal divination in your own era (I've always been nebulous on this point, as you probably are too; how can one tell the true from the false, with as many contradictory accounts as there are in your time?), ignore them at your peril.

A Non-Occurrence at Vyeptos Station

VYEPTOS STATION IS THE SAME as it was in its previous incarnation; a remote listening device, devoid of human inhabitants. It still looks like a silvery insect. As it glides through the eternal night of deep space it diligently and ceaselessly goes about its business of probing, recording, comparing and in general quantifying everything that can possibly be quantified about the physical universe.

The Station is the most reliable, long-lasting data-collector ever created. It's an enormous sensory sponge. And it's about as smart as a sponge, too.

It measures, as it once did, the Gravitational Constant, the Interstitial Electromagnetic Current, the Mean Plasmatic Pressure, the Universal Ionization Factor, the Intergalactic Fog Quotient, and a number of other such details (like the universal Calabi-Yau coupling constant and the non-Higgs field). As before, too, it measures the Total Mass of the Galaxy. It does so countless times in a single period made up of twenty four Standard Galactic Hours (this period is not, as you might expect it to be, a Standard Galactic Day, but rather twenty-four fifths of one). As before, too, it sends out the data it gathers to a plethora of listening posts, where the measurements are archived for future reference.

The Total Mass of the Galaxy is in fact one of the more popular items that's looked up in the pan-planetary database that collects all of the Station's output. Today one of the regular observers pulls up the Total Mass of the Galaxy and responds just in the way that she remembers having done yesterday (an illusion, of course, since this new universe has just been created—but everyone has been created with the history and memories of everything that happened in the previous universe. Information is information.). She nods, smiles, checks off the item from her roster, and goes on to the next one.

She reacts this way because the Total Mass of the Galaxy is constant (within the expected variations of known stellar phenomena, which push the number of atoms up and down just a tad). No trends of mass change outside the normal range is to be reported.

The next item she accesses is a measurement of the current redshift of this particular Galaxy. Here too she nods, smiles, checks off the item from her roster, and proceeds. The Galaxy is moving at the expected speed, and the universe as a whole (it can be inferred from this and other redshift values) is expanding at an accelerating rate that matches current predictions based on previous observations.

Studious and ever-prudent, this researcher decides to play it safe, and confirm her findings directly with Vyeptos Station. She has earned the right, through her title and rank, to ping the Station directly with a query and receive an answer.

She does this now. She asks a question and the Station replies.

This response is sent by the Station in the form of an unencrypted signal that other researchers will be able to access as well, should they want to:

THERE ARE AT PRESENT NO SIGNS OF ANY
GALACTIC MASS DETERIORATION. THIS REMAINS
AT LEVEL ZERO.

ALL REDSHIFT OBSERVATIONS ARE ALSO WITH-
IN EXPECTED RANGES.

HAVE A NICE DAY.

The signal repeats for a period of ten Standard Galactic Hours, the usual amount for such an inquiry.

Various scholars, scientists, artists and bon vivants happen upon the signal, and all of them breathe in, and breathe out, becalmed at the knowledge that the universe continues to tick along predictably—and safely.

Vyeptos Station itself is oblivious of the calming, reassuring influence its mechanical response has exerted. It doesn't care about such things (that final suggestion to have a good day is some hapless Sixth Mandala programmer's idea of polite etiquette, not a manifestation of the Station's sentience).

THE LAST MANDALA SWEEPS

ON EARTH, AT KALAHIDE KEEP, Sinon Kreidge floats, well-rested, in his regeneration field, and ponders the mysteries of existence. To him, now, comes his daughter Kaivilda:

"I've been to the Plain, father. I've heard the Oracles speak."

He fixes his eyes on her with a genuine show of interest as he ascends a few more inches.

Then Sinon eases himself out of the gently meditative state, allows his body to descend back to the ground, and studies Kaivilda fully.

"Go on," he instructs. "What did the Oracles tell you?"

"I'm not sure how it relates to the reports we've been getting," she says, stalling. "But maybe you were right to want to investigate."

"You didn't answer my question, Kaivilda," Sinon says. He raises his voice by a fraction of a decibel when he utters her name; no one else on Earth except for him and his daughter could perceive the subtlety of the shifted inflection.

But it's enough to freeze her in place.

"Yes, father," she says at once. "They have foretold that a woman born of Earthfolk, but not Earthfolk herself, will relinquish her immortality to take to the stars. She must lose herself to find herself."

"What else?" Sinon prods, sensing that there is more.

"And...if she does not do these things, great peril lies in store for Earth."

"Great peril—for Earth?"

"So they said, father," Kaivilda says, disoriented by his surprise. "Does that mean something to you?"

Sinon is quiet. Then he says, "The first part of the prophecy might mean something."

"You think it refers to me, don't you?" she asks, emotion brimming in her voice. "Who else could it be? I'm sure of it!"

"You certainly meet the description," Sinon confirms. "You are a woman born of me, an Earther, but are not one of us."

It is at times like these that Kaivilda feels more lonely, more powerless to control her own fate, than even the lowliest artificial sentient on heavenly, elysian Earth.

"So I must give up my immortality. I must lose myself in that way. But to find myself?" she asks. "What could that possibly mean? My place is here with you."

"Indeed it is," Sinon says, with a twitch of discomfort. "Also, there are no indications of any threat to Earth whatsoever. We have been unmolested for millennia, out of harm's way, with an abundance of riches, and an unending supply of new technologies and services from those who admire us and those who wish to learn from us how to truly vanquish death. So perhaps we're misunderstanding the Oracles' proclamations."

Kaivilda returns to her earlier question. "What do you think they mean when they say that I should take to the stars and find myself?"

Sinon suddenly grows distraught. "Why do you insist on a question you've already answered for yourself?" he says. "It is a meaningless statement."

"You and I both know the Oracles speak the truth," Kaivilda says with growing force. "If we cannot see their meaning the fault is ours, not theirs. They have indicated that I am to find myself. I think you know what lies behind these words," she goes on, surprising herself with the vigor of her conviction, "and you're choosing not to share it with me. Please, father. Please. I must know."

Sinon paces, all signs of his earlier meditative detachment gone. Worry burns through his features, and his body language denotes, alternately, resentment and shame. Sinon loves his daughter more than anything else in life—even his own immortality. But it is not a pure, unconditional love; he expects something in return. He draws his strength from knowing that he can depend on her always, come what may. He draws his pride from knowing that he has fashioned an individual of undying loyalty, of limitless dedication. At times, he has forced himself to examine the contradiction in these sentiments, the absurdity of cherishing the adulation of someone who adulates him only because they were made to do so, because they are too afraid to do otherwise. How can it be a celebration of his freedom, an assertion of his independence and control over the dominion of his life, to hold to his bosom a hostage, a prisoner of his devotion? How can he truly be a master if the one whom he cherishes is a slave by design? The pain of these thoughts, during the instances when he has had the courage to crystallize them, has left him wrecked for days, a jangled mess of depression and lack of self-worth. Relief tends to wash over him after the self-loathing finally wears off, and when the relief passes, the sensation is gratifying, cleansing, even better than the fake arrogance with which he usually struts around.

All of this comes roiling forth now. The Oracles' words have confronted him with the ugliest side of himself, and he has no place to hide.

"I think it can only possibly mean one thing," he says, at last, voice breaking. "It means that you must assert your independence. It means that you must free yourself of me. It means that I must finally relinquish my hold over you, and learn to live my life as it once was, unblemished by your captivity."

He breaks down then. Kaivilda approaches him cautiously. Her instincts shout out that she must comfort him. But there is an ugly honesty to the words he has uttered that leaves her petrified, mortally afraid to step even an inch closer to this megalomaniacal man.

She is as much to blame as him, she realizes, as she contemplates his frame, shuddering with guilt, heaving with remorse. She has never found the strength within herself, until now, to admit the truth of her situation. She has been kept a prisoner in this place, yes. She has been captive; commanded to do thus and thus; mortified of the very notion of displeasing her father—her creator—the one who has had *absolute* power over her. She has had no rights. But, rights or no rights, she has ceded her very need to have rights, and it is this loss that has cast her adrift, that has filled her life with unhappiness. No matter how much she pleases Sinon she can never please herself. She must please herself *for herself*; and if *that* pleases Sinon, too, very well, so be it.

"You are right," she says, still tempted to come to his rescue, but still pinned in place by her fears of succumbing once more to her own learned responses of subservience, of the need to please. "I must leave you. I must find my own way. And the cost for departing Earth is that I will no longer be able to live indefinitely."

"If the reports are true, you will not be able to rebirth either," Sinon says, the graveness of the realization stunning him into a semblance of composure.

"Then this will be my last life, as I am now," Kaivilda says, the words sounding less unreal in her ears than she might have expected. For any other Earth-dweller it would seem unthinkable, to live merely a few centuries and then die—a travesty of the perceived order of things, of the mandate to live on and on and on and experience everything in a million different ways. But for her, subject as she has been to the constant fear that Sinon might grow weary of her, that he might at any moment, on a whim, find no use for her and choose to discontinue her existence, for her it's a different story. No day has been taken for granted; every new dawn has been an education, replete with longing, gratitude at her continued existence, and desperate uncertainty about the future. To unshackle herself from such an unstable predicament is not to sentence herself to an abnormally short lifespan or to cheat herself out of a vast life that's rightfully hers. On the contrary, it is to guarantee her future, to ensure that the few centuries she has are truly *hers*, to do with as she pleases. "This will be my last life," she repeats. "Yes. And the first that is my very own. I shall endeavor to make the most of it."

Sinon is well on the way to overcoming his own flush of emotions. She sees in his demeanor that he has found some truth within that he is using to prop himself back up, to rebuild himself.

With a sincerity that is almost startling, Sinon says, "Kaivilda, I shouldn't have waited this long. I shouldn't have needed an Oracle to tell me what to do, and to threaten peril to the Earth. I know what is wrong and what is right. Since the moment I created you out of dust, I have been vicious and controlling. I was abusive even when I was polite and pleasant, for there was always an undercurrent of complete domination. I am deeply ashamed and troubled by what I have done. I am more sorry than you can ever conceive. But it's done; I can't take it back. What I can say is that I have no doubt that your life, starting from this moment, will be a full one, and that your kindness and patience will bring joy to whomever you choose to share them with. The Oracles have singled you out for a reason, and though we don't know the nature of your destiny, don't ever forget that you have one. You, my daughter," and here he is overwhelmed again, and muddles through with great difficulty, "you, my daughter, are a creature of light, and you will shine brightly wherever you go. You are the finest, fairest, most beautiful creation of all Earth, and the Earth will be dimmed when you take flight, even if in so doing you save us all."

"Father, I will never forget you," Kaivilda says, drawing near. "And I shall always be grateful that you breathed life into my atoms, and made me who I am."

Those are Kaivilda's parting words.

Sinon feels bittersweet and conflicted later that day. He is happy for Kaivilda, but an old controlling part of him clings on still, and that part is saddened by the improvement in her lot; her good fortune is, in some regard, Sinon's loss. He feels now that close cousin of *Schadenfreude*, *Freudenschade*.

Later, in the evening, the *Freudenschade* abandons him, its gummy residue fading fast, replaced by elation, an exhilarating sense of accomplishment that rinses his emotional palate clean. By nighttime, with Kaivilda gone, truly gone, her absence, so prominent, so tangible in every chamber of his grand castle, triggers a deep, irresistible weariness within Sinon.

He must rest.

Earthfolk, like just about everyone else in the Ninth Mandala, have no need for sleep, no need for recuperation, for their bodies are self-sustaining, their minds capable of uninterrupted operation (though they enjoy escaping from pure consciousness once in a while into various modalities of wakeful dreaming).

But for the first time in his incomprehensibly enormous lifespan, Sinon feels the need to shut himself down completely, to truly surrender to the oblivion of sleep.

Sleep! A frightening word, once. The same as death. But he is not frightened now. He is too exhausted for fear, too numb to feel anything but the immediate need for even more numbing nothingness.

My purpose is complete, Sinon thinks as he enters the deepest rest he has ever experienced, one so profound he did not think it was possible.

His awareness of his own body melts away. His consciousness tunnels out of himself and into a grand, infinite void, where all is quiet, peaceful—and cold, starkly and penetratingly cold.

He likes it. He feels welcomed by the unending expanse of chilled night.

He belongs here.

At last. At last. At last.

Perhaps I can stay here for a time, he thinks—and that, as it turns out, is Sinon Kreidge's final thought—and then he sleeps, he sleeps as never before, and does not awaken.

THE LAST MANDALA SWEEPS, CONTINUED

HANOSZ PRIME, ABSOLUTE MONARCH and undisputed ruler of Prime, is also tired (though in a different way than Sinon, whom in this universe he has never met, and never will). Hanosz has in truth been tired for some time, but the business of rebirth is not a trivial one—especially if he is to believe the latest gossip—and he has been putting it off.

The weariness, however, is beginning to manifest in ways that he can no longer ignore, even with his practiced repertoire of suppression techniques and his artful self-deception. The tiredness lies within his mind, inside the very intangible processes that help him form thoughts, particularly those thoughts that lend meaning to the words *purpose* and *future*. He is spiritually depleted, existentially cranky, and he must attend to these needs before he gets himself in serious trouble.

Then too, his apocalyptic memories have been returning. He thought they might have been visions, at first, or merely dreams—but there is something distinctly *past* about them. They ring within his mind as echoes, not divinations or portents. He can't explain why he's convinced that they're memories, since they portray the destruction, among other things, of Prime itself, and clearly no such event has ever unfolded. But they are memories nonetheless (perhaps someone else's?) and their ever more frequent intrusions into his conscious existence will soon wreak havoc with his kingdom, with his ability to function even on a basic level, if he does not put an end to them.

Very well. No more stalling. He must replenish his spirit and make himself alive inside; he must undergo rebirth; he can no longer wait.

And yet—there are disturbing rumors—

"Hanosz, my king," one of his noblemen intrudes, as though anticipating the monarch's intent. "I have obtained the information you requested. I realize that you asked Gheimeh Orr to look into this matter for you, and that you asked that it be handled with the utmost discretion, but Gheimeh has fallen ill and has asked me to convey the message on his behalf."

The nobleman looks tentative. It takes Hanosz only a few instants to recognize him, based on his shifty posture and dubitative demeanor; one Kashk O'Bademjan. He is one of the old guard, noblemen and courtiers who served Hanosz's father (and, history says, served him well), thereby earning the reward of assured employment into the next generation. Gheimeh is of the old guard, too, even more aged than Kashk, but more friendly, efficient, and trustworthy. Or so Hanosz thought until now. This turn of events makes Hanosz suspect that though Gheimeh may be loyal, he is also cowardly, and has feigned some medical condition to avoid the unpleasant task of reporting out on his findings. This, in turn, means that his findings will surely be less then consoling. Hanosz is annoyed. One nobleman whom Hanosz thought he could rely on has proven himself to be averse to conflict, and has suckered in an even more incompetent specimen to complete his task for him.

Hanosz, in a passive sort of way, has never cared for Kashk, but in the current moment he actively dislikes him.

Hanosz says, with more than a hint of impatience, "And what have you found?"

"My lord," Kashk chirrups, in the high-pitched deferential way that Hanosz has come to detest, "I'm afraid the news is not good."

"That explains the expression of unabashed mirth on your countenance, and why you're here instead of Gheimeh. Please give him my regards, by the way. I hope that when he recovers his nerve—I mean health—it will aid him in the search for a new job. Now go on."

Kashk attempts to strike an officious pose, and falls short. "Every documented instance of rebirthing that has been attempted during the last week or so, on all known worlds, has inexplicably failed."

"In what way?"

Kashk seems to wonder whether it's a trick question, and seems to be mentally reviewing whatever information Gheimeh has passed on to him. "The person undergoing the procedure did not emerge any younger."

"Well of course they didn't!" Hanosz snaps. "The word 'failed' seems to make that part rather clear, don't you think? But did those who attempted the procedure *survive*? There are, after all, many kinds of failure, and in that spectrum of undesirable contingencies, upholding the status quo of aged living seems infinitely less undesirable than dying."

"Yes, of course," Kashk says, and nods, though Hanosz is not sure, from the dolt's vague gesture and slowness of movement, what the nodding is supposed to convey. "In a few cases, the subject did indeed suffer irreparable damage, but in most he or she simply emerged without any change at all."

"What else?"

"That is all," Kashk replies.

"This is what took you almost a week to ascertain? Where are the details, the documents, the cross-examinations? Where is the summary of your analysis containing your personal opinion regarding the degree of trustworthiness of these reports?"

"I apologize, my king," Kashk manages, even more awkwardly than usual, "I did not realize you were looking for such a thorough investigation. I will compile all my findings immediately and have them to you within the hour."

"Kashk," Hanosz says, enjoying the unnerving effect on his servant that comes from this use of his first name, "going forward, whenever we are assessing something that entails direct risk to me, I would appreciate it if you would assume that the highest degree of thoroughness is expected in your research. Moreover when the risk might be the termination of my life."

"Yes, of course."

"Now get to it."

Kashk slinks away from Hanosz's presence, leaving a faint whiff of incompetence in his wake.

An hour and twenty impatient minutes later Hanosz receives the prompt for a data-spore in the connector embedded in his body-modularity, and when he sees Kashk's signature he accepts it. It takes Hanosz only a few misery-laden minutes to pore through Gheimeh's poorly organized findings, as made even less organized by Kashk. There's no need to delve into the data deeply, and no choice but to arrive at the obvious conclusion. It is as the old nobleman has informed him; no rebirth has wrought the desired effect, and in about fifteen percent of all cases rebirth has resulted in death.

He scans the data again. What's this, a side note? Ah, yes. Of course. He should have suspected as much. *Earth*, of all places, seems to be unaffected by this bizarre collapse of the rebirthing science. Earth is blessed with unique sunlight and air which, combined with an improved rejuvenation technique, still seems to support unlimited rebirths. Good for them. Perhaps, Hanosz muses, he ought to pay the planet a visit. Though he's not sure, on second thought, that it would do him a lot of good: to begin with, he is not of Earth descent, and, to continue, the effect is localized and would presumably only take hold if he elected to remain there (which he has no intention of doing). In addition, the Earth-kin must surely be taking measures to protect their secret, lest they become inundated with folks from all over the Galaxy demanding an Earthly rebirth, or worse, seeking permanent relocation.

No. Whatever Hanosz decides to do, it must be without the help of Earth.

The first order of business is clear.

He must attempt a rebirth here on Prime.

The data claims that failure is inevitable, and death possible. But if he does nothing, death is inevitable. So he risks very little by trying.

He gives the order at once and preparations are summarily made. Only his brother attempts to talk him out of it (presumably because he does not wish to face the responsibility of having to take over, if Hanosz were to perish—or is Hanosz being too harsh on his sibling?). He makes it clear that he is going to proceed anyway, and proceed he does.

Within an hour of his decision he finds himself entering the nutrient-enhanced rebirth tank, and suspending his mind into the state that is recommended for the changes to wash over him.

He notices a prickling sensation all over his body that he didn't experience in his previous rebirth. It is followed by a rash of pain that seems to spread from within, igniting his nerve endings with discomfort. It passes, and then nothing happens for a time.

After that, he returns to full-fledged consciousness, prompted by the operator's signal, and he is informed that the procedure did not work.

"At least I'm still here," Hanosz mutters.

Once he is out of the chamber he summons Captain Tio Patcnact to his palace. Patcnact's specialty is Hanosz's ship, of course, but he has proven useful in the past with other matters involving information that goes beyond the Parasol system.

Hanosz beams a summary of everything he has learned so far, and his own failed recent rebirth attempt, to Patcnact's data connector, and then asks, "What are your thoughts regarding this mess? Can you cross-check these reports against whatever news you've been monitoring from other worlds?"

Patcnact says without hesitation, "I can."

"And to what would you attribute this sudden, widespread inability to achieve rebirth?"

Patcnact is thoughtful. "The phenomenon is widespread, as you say, so the mechanism that causes it may be galactic, or even universal, in origin. I hesitate to speculate about how such a phenomenon could arise. One thing seems relatively clear, though. Our understanding of the rebirth process suggests that, under normal circumstances, it eventually becomes less than perfect because of a buildup of solar poisons. It stands to reason, then, that such a buildup may have been accelerated, and all over the galaxy at once—perhaps all over the cosmos."

"Can the levels of solar poisons be directly measured?" Hanosz inquires.

"I'm afraid not. The levels of background radiation can, of course, and solar flux is easy to detect as well, but the solar poisons are more elusive, as they result from the interaction of these radiations with the energy field generated by living creatures. This field can only be apprehended indirectly."

"Why couldn't we arrange to measure *my* energy field," Hanosz says rapidly, "and *my* level of solar poisons, and ascertain whether your hypothesis holds true for me?"

"That we could," Patcnact says. He pauses.

"What troubles you, old friend?"

"What will you do if we confirm that it is the solar poisons, Hanosz? There is no known way to eliminate them, for that would mean reducing the background radiation of the universe as a whole. You would know, then, that this life is to be your last."

"Your directness is appreciated, as always," Hanosz says.

"I notice that you have not answered my question."

"I have no answer at this time," Hanosz replies. "Whatever the reality of the situation is, I must learn to live with it. If rebirthing is no longer an option—for me, or for anyone else—a great many things will have to change for our society and our worlds to be able to continue to function. It's exhausting to think about."

"Then perhaps you should rest your mind," Patcnact suggests. "You've had a trying day."

"I have a feeling my days are about to get a lot more trying," Hanosz says, smiling bitterly.

"I'm here, and happy to help however I can," Patcnact says, realizing that their conversation is drawing to a close.

"Thank you," Hanosz says. And then a curtain of silence falls upon him, deep and stifling, and Patcnact takes his leave.

Poor Hanosz, indeed.

Not only is our hero tired now; he's weighed down by the immediacy of his mortality. If he had been able, at least, to get in one more rebirth before the process went awry, he would have bought himself at least another century of life, and he would have started off invigorated, flexible, ready to adapt to life's needs.

But as it is now, he has decades left, at the most—decades in which, in his current environment, he feels stultified and stagnant. Unnecessary. Is this the most that he can look forward to, simply waiting out his own decline, trying not to make a complete fool of himself as his mental faculties begin to break down?

So much for playing a key role in the universe. (Of course, other than his confusing memory-dreams of the apocalypse, Hanosz has no recollection that his previous version actually saved the universe. And even if he did, we ought to wonder how much that would cheer him up in his current state. Maybe it would make him feel even more impotent.) In Hanosz's new universe, there is no hypersingularity, and so there have been no prophecies regarding his role in the eventual rescue of the All.

But in the universe in which his previous self completed such a rescue, there had been a foretelling on Prime that a member of the Prime family would "meet his end at the beginning of time, but that he would emerge with godlike nature."

As with all such foretellings, we can only see their truth post facto. For consider the propositions in reverse order: Hanosz has indeed emerged in this universe with godlike nature.

Godlike how? you ask. He can't even keep himself alive!

Well, sure, be glib—but Hanosz *has* emerged with the godlike nature of having saved the universe by having preserved its information content (whether he knows it or not is irrelevant).

And now consider the remaining claim, that Hanosz was to meet his end at the beginning of time.

Isn't that exactly what's happening? In the infancy of this new universe (though to all who inhabit it, it seems to have been around for billions of years, and they all have the memories and historical archives to "prove" it, we know that this is an illusion, for they were merely recreated this way)—in other words, at the beginning of time—Hanosz finds himself incapable of further rebirths. It's the end of the line for him and for everyone else (except for the glorious Earth-born).

And so he is to meet his end at the beginning of time.

—But remember, there's been a new prophecy, concerning Kaivilda this time. Our story wouldn't be complete without following it to its natural conclusion.

Hanosz has been mulling over his fate for the last couple of days and he has resolved that he will go down fighting. He will set out on his ship to explore the cause of the mysterious increase in solar poisons, and wherever this line of investigation takes him, he'll pursue it up to the very end.

The solar poison effect, after all, is a physical one, and it must therefore be susceptible to empirical analysis. Hanosz has not been trained in the ways of science, for such a training would have been wasted on a monarch. But he vows now to remedy all the gaps in his knowledge via information downloads and accelerated tutelage from the best analysts and theoreticians at his disposal.

This is easier thought than done.

The work turns out to be mentally tedious, and even as he assumes a highly regimented, disciplinarian approach to the skills he wishes to master, a part of Hanosz (a loud one) asks whether he isn't going about this the wrong way. As the difficulty—and abstruseness—of the subject matters increase, so do his self-doubts. Is this really the best way to spend my remaining years? Hanosz asks myself. Lost amidst a sea of symbols and hypotheses? Casting about in space, as I no doubt will, in search for something that may never be found and, if it is located, might never be understood?

He presses on, quashing his doubts, reminding himself that his mind is frail with age, that it cannot be trusted, that his weakness is a byproduct of exhaustion, not rational argument.

The lessons become challenging indeed, incomprehensible after a while, and he finds that he must slow down his pace, backtrack, repeat what he has already learned. The theory underlying the solar poisons makes a child out of him, reducing him to his most basic constituents, rendering his limitations more obvious than ever before. Hanosz's tutors are patient to a fault, and still he makes little progress. He despairs then. A sinking, hopeless feeling takes over. He comes to believe that he has cornered himself into an activity from which he derives no pleasure and to which there is no end in sight (he has centuries of subject matter to dominate, after all, if he wants to be brought up to speed on the nuances of the latest findings and theories—and even with Ninth Mandala learning techniques it still takes *time*, spades of it, to assimilate such an elaborate edifice of abstraction.)

One day, after a particularly insufferable lesson, he decides to call it quits.

I will burn my dreams at the pyre of my own inadequacy, he thinks with sullenness, and makes himself ready for defeat.

But his teacher, a virtual sentient by the name of Thol Vredes, rescues him, gently but firmly prodding him on, enticing him with his pride, astutely manipulating what remains of his ego, strengthening his confidence.

This teetering on the brink of failure continues for many days, but at last Hanosz believes himself prepared for the voyage to the stars that will put his hard-learned knowledge to the test, and at last his advisors and instructors agree that he has mastered the fundamentals, and that his journey will not be a waste of time.

Two days before his scheduled departure he allows his mind to enter an unusually long regenerative state, hoping it will repair some of the thought-turbulence he has been battling of late. He notices that he is not besieged by the usual apocalyptic memory-dreams. *Perhaps I'm simply too drained*, he thinks, *or my mind has become too crammed with other things.* He doesn't question it further, and enjoys the quiet.

On the morning that his expedition is to launch, an entourage of courtiers and nobles approaches him. Hanosz imagines, naively, that they have come to talk him out of his wild scheme. Or perhaps they've come to wish him luck, for they cannot be rid of him soon enough.

He's ready, either way.

Both guesses prove to be wrong.

Kashk O'Bademjan is the first to speak, in his slimy, ingratiating way. "Lord Prime," he says pompously, "we did our best to shield you, but we failed."

The others nod grimly.

"What are you talking about?" Hanosz demands. "Shield me from what?"

"We pointed out that you were indisposed, making preparations for a trip. We explained that you might not be back anytime soon, if at all," Kashk goes on.

"But your guest chose not to listen," one of the other noblemen continues. "The virtuals onboard the visitor's ship somehow disabled our protective measures. I'm afraid your privacy won't last much longer."

"We're sorry," Kashk says.

"Who are you talking about? I've authorized no guests, granted no visitors a royal audience."

"As we are well aware," one of Hanosz's guards says. "That's why we wanted to warn you in person."

"Well, who in the blazes is it?" Hanosz insists. "Someone I know?"

And at that precise moment the air before him shimmers with the materialization of a new presence.

Hanosz takes several steps back, and his guards form a defensive perimeter around him. But it's nothing more than a formality, for if the intruder has made it this far into Hanosz's inner sanctum, his guards won't serve as an effective barrier.

Hanosz performs the equivalent of a blink.

Time seems to slow down, then start back up—then slow down again.

He has seen this person before, though he doesn't know how or where.

She has appeared in his dreams, perhaps; in some previous life, if he is to accept that his visions are indeed memories.

It doesn't matter.

He is entranced.

Click whisper his modularity and his identity, both at once!

This is it! *Click*!

She is a creature more alluring, more perfectly serene, than he has ever seen. She draws him to her with the strength of nothing less than a singularity. The attraction is irresistible, dictated by the laws of space and time itself.

She advances toward him too. He signals the guards to disperse, and they do so at once.

The elegance and sleekness of her gliding movement is paralleled only by the unbroken contours and ovoid symmetry of her crystalline modularity.

Hanosz is stunned.

"I am Kaivilda, of Earth," the visitor announces.

Hanosz struggles to break free of the muteness imposed upon him by Kaivilda's beauty, barely managing to speak.

"I am Hanosz Prime, of Prime," he says simply.

***

The entire universe has been refashioned only weeks ago, but for Hanosz and Kaivilda, who have no recollection of this, and indeed live within a universe whose recorded history stretches back for billions and billions of years—just think, over one hundred mandalas!—this objective truth is immaterial. Their newfound rapport, vibrant and irresistible, makes the universe subjectively new in a way that no amount of matter and energy reshuffling could ever hope to match.

Kaivilda and Hanosz have entered into full rapport. It doesn't take long, either. A few days on Prime are enough for them to realize that, whatever other vicissitudes life has in store for them, they are destined to face them together.

I attempted to convey their rapport once before in terms of negations, speaking of things like prunes and plans, death and war and responsibility, freedom and temptation.

But this current rapport is so intense, so perfect, so impossibly whole and all-consuming, that it makes the previous rapport look like the tentative, clumsy fumbling of two twenty-first century teenagers. *This* rapport cannot be expressed in terms of a remainder, for it encompassed All of Creation. *This* rapport includes everything that Is, connecting everything that was once apart, joining and unifying even the most disparate of forces, sensations, impressions and ideas. *This* rapport is impurity made pure; this rapport clearly marks the end of one thing and the beginning of another, and there is no bridge between the before and after except for the rapport itself. *This* rapport holds every imaginable contradiction in its arms, and pats them on the shoulder. *This* rapport casts roots that stretch backward in time through the earliest instant of Hanosz's and Kaivilda's awareness, all the way forward in time to their very last breath.

This rapport, in short, contains within it infinity itself.

And with that infinity Hanosz takes stock of his situation in a new way, and abandons his plans to investigate the cause of the solar poisons increase among the stars.

Rapport is, after all, change. And Hanosz finds himself changed indeed.

He has been confronting the problem of his mortality and the solar poisons in the wrong way. He shouldn't go gallivanting around in space on what will surely turn out to be a wild goose chase.

He should stay where he is and enjoy every moment that is left to him.

Hanosz accepts his mortality.

Think of Kaivilda, he tells himself. *If she has been willing to forgo her immortality to come here and find me, can't I, too, accept my own passing?*

Is it such a terrible fate? He will rule over Prime with Kaivilda at his side for whatever time he has left. She herself has suggested this arrangement, and it fills Hanosz with joy.

Hanosz, Hanosz tells himself, using his own name as though it were that of a stranger, *you will die. You will end. Everyone who is not on Earth dies, and everything that is not of Earth ends. Nothing can be done about it. You have decades left, with luck. And that is fine. It is as it must be; it is as it should be. You will die, and that is that. But right now, you are alive, and that too is fine. Quite fine! And that too is as it must be, as it should be. You will die; but first, you will live. So live! You have earned the right to live, by staying alive until now. Live. Live.*

Hanosz accepts the order of things.

Kaivilda speaks to him of the celebration of her own newfound freedom. They are both free now for the first time, despite the finality of the death that awaits them.

Yes, Hanosz thinks.

This is the last mandala whose sweep he will witness. That *they* will witness.

It's an oddly beautiful thought.

THE GRAND CIRCULARITY OF EVERYTHING

AH YES, GOOD FOR HANOSZ. It had to end this way. (Of course, I knew this from the start. I did my best not to ruin the surprise.) I'm sure you're just as glad as I am that he has decided to settle down. Imagine the alternative; he begins to snoop around for the cause of the minutely elevated radiation levels that have ruined the delicate balance of forces that permit rebirthing, and in the process he inadvertently causes some Universe-threatening havoc all over again, and off we go, dashing into the mad chaos of singularities and collapsing worlds and blue-shifting galaxies!

No, no, we can't have that (at least not again). Hanosz will no longer give much thought to the mystery of the increased solar poisons, for he will find contentment in the company of Kaivilda. And if he doesn't worry about it, neither should you.

There is another question, though, that may be irking you, you back there in your home-world of Earth that is (as you now know) to be destroyed and recreated in the unimaginably distant future.

And that is the question of *me*.

Who am *I*? To whom belongs the voice that has sung to you of Hanosz Prime's tale?

It's not an illogical question, and it's not an impertinent one, either. I take no offense at being dragged directly into this. After all, that was the risk I took the very first time I used the word *I*. I accept the consequences of such an identification. I'll share with you what you wish to know (but I won't repeat it, and I won't say it loudly either, for I would rather that it stay just between the two of us).

So listen closely.

You know about the Earth natives. You know that they alone have escaped the fate to which all other beings have succumbed in this reconstructed Universe. Only Earth-dwellers are immune from the elevated levels of solar poisons; only they can live forever, in the strict sense of the word.

And live forever they do (though not Sinon, of course, who has voluntarily dissolved himself in the Great Sleep). The creatures of Earth last indefinitely, rejuvenating themselves, continuing to accrue experiences and knowledge all the while, and developing patterns of behavior that, with the passing of the mandalas, eventually become incomprehensible to anyone *not* from Earth. The Earth beings evolve social practices and modes of communication so sophisticated and abstract as to make contact with non-Earthers either impractical or unnecessary.

Eventually, the Earth goes silent.

Envoys from other worlds (including a small scarlet teardrop ship from the Parasol system populated with the far-removed descendants of Hanosz Prime) are sent to Earth to investigate. They are profoundly befuddled, for they find the entire planet deserted. Sure, virtuals and other creatures like the Oracles remain behind, but the Earthers are gone and there doesn't appear to be any farewell message. The visitors investigate but find nothing. With much chagrin, they return to their native planets, bearing the strange and sad news. The Earthers may not have perished, but they might as well have, as far as anyone else is concerned.

The true fate of the Earth beings takes a long time to be revealed—time on a scale so vast that mandalas themselves become little more than the blink of an eye—but it *is* revealed in time, and in a manner which proves to be most unpleasant for everyone else.

Recall that, back in the year 777 of Cycle 888 of the 1111th Encompassment of the Ninth Mandala of a previous universe, a veritable cornucopia of body-modularities was available to the Earthers, who did not hesitate to don even the most farfetched of these physical manifestations. Recall too that the ability to exist without a modularity altogether—the true disembodied form—had been a viable option, though it was a minority taste. Now fast forward to the reassembled Universe, and skip forward thousands of Encompassments, jump by a dozen mandalas, a thousand mandalas, and keep on going until you reach the moment in time in which the Earth-natives decide that a disembodied existence is the *only* way to go, and *everyone* on Earth adopts this proposition wholeheartedly. In fact, they take this new fashion so seriously that they make corporeality itself punishable by exile. (There are some who renege initially but in the end they all succumb to this sweeping infatuation with a modularity-free existence.) It begins, as I've just pointed out, in the form of fashion, but quickly grows into something quite different—and with good reason.

Flinging themselves through the cosmos without a physical carapace, the Earth beings discover the ability to reproduce with just a thought. Linked, as they are by now, through an interdimensional network that can exchange vast information in infinitesimal time, they are not dependent on additional units of consciousness like themselves to function. But they envision an even greater potential for connectedness, one in which every atom of the physical Universe is inhabited by a non-physical information-processing entity, all of them sharing Everything at the Same Time. To reach this end (which you might think of as oppressive, claustrophobic even, but which they envision in romantic terms) they begin to spawn copies of themselves at an unprecedented rate, and these copies multiply even faster. These floating, non-corporeal descendants of the original body-free Earthers literally become countless.

Possessing the ability to alter physical reality with their non-physical thoughts, they decide, one day, that there's really no point in having so much *stuff* in the Universe.

What good, after all, are neutron stars and interstellar clouds and asteroid belts and planetary rings and icy comets and binary systems and even, for that matter, other living beings who are still shackled to repellent bodies? Everything in the Universe becomes ugly to these beings; mere clutter.

With a single thought, they remedy that state of affairs, emptying the entire Universe of everything physical. (This is the unfortunate moment when all other sentient beings wink out of existence.)

They then transform all of this into energy, energy which they re-invest directly into the creation of even more copies of themselves. In other words, they consume the entire contents of the cosmos and then smother the empty space that remains behind. But this is just the start of the Reassembly.

Once all matter is gone, they have to learn to deal with the energy of empty space itself, a vast and powerful force, and when they master its secrets they do the same as before, tapping this energy and siphoning it from space so that even *that* is gone.

At this time, quite literally nothing except themselves remains.

Completely merged, and defining the totality of existence, these beings have now literally *become* the Universe.

The whole shebang is therefore now conscious and self-aware.

I am that Universe.

At various times during our song, I have pretended to be of your time and space, so that you might have more easily identified with the meaning I was attempting to convey. The truth is, you and I are nothing alike.

Naturally, the universe (me), having reached this state of unsurpassable elegance, knowledge and all-encompassing minimalist beauty, grows bored now and again.

The universe therefore decides to tell itself stories to pass the time.

The tale of Hanosz Prime was one such story (and at least partially true, at that!).

Don't judge me unfavorably because of this inclination; storytelling is a noble tradition. And even if it weren't...well, everyone needs to do *something*.

Heigh-ho! Heigh-ho! It has been fun to sing of the ending of time!

Heigh-ho!

And now we turn to a different song—

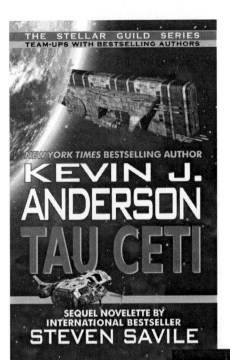

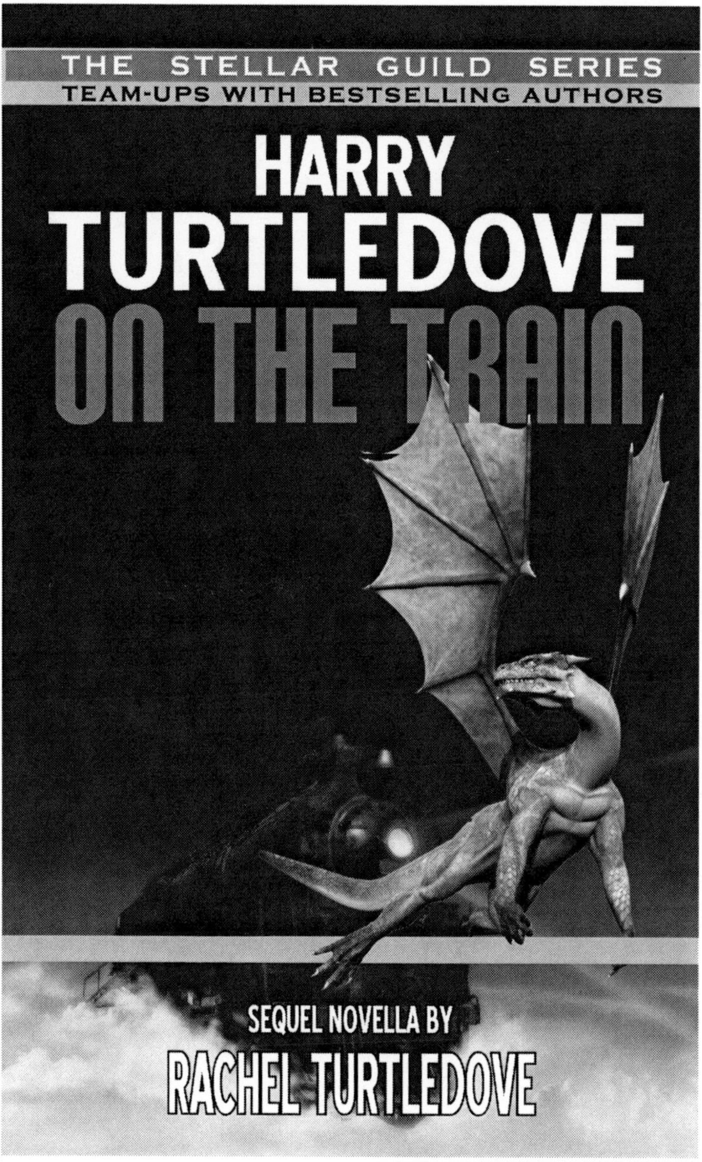
THE STELLAR GUILD SERIES
TEAM-UPS WITH BESTSELLING AUTHORS
HARRY TURTLEDOVE
ON THE TRAIN
SEQUEL NOVELLA BY
RACHEL TURTLEDOVE

CPSIA information can be obtained at www.ICGtesting.com
Printed in the USA
LVOW041746301112

309542LV00001B/48/P